The Gypsy Caravan

Susanna Scott

ISBN: 9798739721303

For my Family

Chapter 1

Two hundred and fifty miles of torrential rain and powerful gusts of wind all the way – and you wait until now? Sadie peered in exasperation at the sunshine, which had tentatively appeared near the end of her journey. She could finally prise her fingers from the steering wheel, unclench her teeth and stop doing Quasimodo impressions while squinting through the almost opaque windscreen. The journey north had required all her concentration. Now though in the valley to her left, the watery sun dappled the lush green slopes, its rays highlighting the stand of trees nestling there.

Sadie yawned loudly and pulled her mud-splattered car to the side of the road. She pulled the rear-view mirror towards her and surveyed a baggy-eyed insomnia victim with a lunchtime tomato sauce splodge on her top lip and a fringe sticking straight up in fright after running her hands through it so many times. She managed a half-grin. Here I come folks, ready or not she, thought- but from what she remembered, the wilds of Yorkshire welcomed everyone – freaky hairstyle or not. She pulled out a tissue to get rid of the possible road-kill appearance of her top lip though. There were limits.

Needing to stretch her legs and take in the beautiful surroundings, she stepped out into the shimmering yet subdued heat. It was almost as though she had left the grey misery behind and driven towards the welcoming sun. Grinning at the analogy between the journey's weather conditions and her life, she looked around.

Down below her, the valley stretched to the right as far as the eye could see. An ethereal mist hung above the ground, rising from the wet grass where the warmth was hitting it; the aftermath of a Spring storm. A few farms were dotted about on the slopes but at the end of the valley, nestling comfortably, as it had done for hundreds of years, was the small village of Brytherstone.

Sadie had fond memories of holidays spent here with her mad Aunt Em. They were a much-needed retreat from all the bustle and bile of the city she had lived in then and from the strict rules and regulations of her workaholic parents. If only they had known their rules had no place here... Their apparently nervous daughter climbed high trees, squelched in mud, stayed outside until dark and raced full pelt down steep hills, breathless and laughing. At first, she was just rebelling against all the things she wasn't allowed to do at home but then it was just for the sheer enjoyment of the freedom she had found. She doubted her parents would have cared what happened at these times; she thought later, because she was someone else's responsibility for a while. Although calling her aunt responsible was, frankly, pushing it.

A car trundled past her and she checked her watch. That same mad aunt would be waiting for her now – and once again, she was providing a much-needed retreat.

*

Em squawked loudly as she surveyed the mountains of sundry items that seemed to be attacking her living room. She had meant to tidy and clean the place before Sadie arrived but had

– and she grudgingly admitted it was inevitable – got side-tracked in her studio. Her short, greying hair, still with rebellious red streaks, was stuck at right angles to her ears and her fringe was in her eyes. She was now covered in a fine layer of white dust and the house-cleaning fairies had failed to materialise yet again. More frantic shoving of things into cupboards so they would fall out again when opened. More flicking, just moving the dust from one surface to disperse on another, a quick collection of dirty plates and cups, which she could hide in the bowl. She ran the hot tap and put plenty of washing-up liquid in to cover the evidence.

Em flew back into the living room, nearly treading on the whisky-coloured ball of fluff, masquerading as a Cairn terrier who was trying to appear invisible in the face of all this unusual and scary cleaning activity.

As Em steadied herself on the door jamb, she caught sight of a photo of Sadie and herself - Sadie aged about twelve – on the sideboard. They had huge grins on their faces with their hair looking like they'd been pulled through a hedge backwards – twice – and they looked so happy and relaxed. She smiled, stopped her cleaning attempts, turned back to the kitchen and went to the fridge. Taking out a bottle of wine, she grabbed two miraculously clean glasses from the drainer. Sadie had loved coming here, accepting Em and her house just as they were. Unless she had changed very much, she would accept things as they were once again.

It was at this point, bottle and glasses in Em's hands that Sadie made her entrance and took in the scene.

'I see nothing has changed since I last saw you then, although there's only one bottle this time…' Sadie laughed.

Em winked. 'The other bottle's in the fridge.'

Then Em put the bottle down and they hugged each other so warmly and so tightly that she feared for the only two clean glasses in the house. As they stepped back, Sadie looked down.

'Whisky!' she yelled and bent down to hug the little dog who couldn't conceal his joy at seeing her again, 'You haven't forgotten me then?'

At these words, she looked guiltily up at the figure above her.

'I'm so sorry Em. I know it's been three years. There's… there's been a lot of 'stuff' going on.'

'Well Sadie Norwood, you're here now and that's all that matters.'

Sadie grinned at her aunt's use of her mother's maiden name and that of Em's herself, as she had never married. Sadie's name was Barnes but she didn't correct her. Norwood sounded nice and somehow more part of the family.

Her aunt saw Sadie still looked as lovely as ever with her high cheekbones and long deep auburn hair but she took in the green eyes that had lost their sparkle, the slumped shoulders, even the lack of the vitality that usually characterised her niece, and picked the bottle up again.

'We have wine and two weeks to talk. You can start now if you want?'

'The wine or the talk?' grinned Sadie.

'Both' answered her aunt.

Chapter 2

Austin was the greyest, dullest man it has ever been my displeasure to meet. He was the most boring man out of many, many boring examples I have met. He could make Isaac Spurling's 'How to sit still and very quiet by a river for hours while hoping a fish will accidentally snag itself on your fishing line' seem interesting by comparison.'

There was a pause.

'You didn't like Austin then Em...? Sadie grinned.

'I'm sorry if I've given you that impression', Em raised an eyebrow.

'...but he *was* the M.P. for the Clayport district and was very knowledgeable on politics.'

'As I said, the most boring man I've ever known'.

Sadie laughed at Em. Even up to a year ago, she'd have tried to stand up for her fiancé but now, well, she felt a great pleasure in admitting that yes, he was the most boring bastard on this Earth! She held her glass forward for another refill.

'What on earth did you see in him? He was tall and lanky with slick-backed hair – what was left of it. His eyes were too small and too close together and he had about as much sex appeal as Eeyore. I can't understand it.'

Sadie took another slurp. She would have to slow down. Maybe.

'Okay, you remember Bob, the boyfriend before Austin?'

'Vaguely. I do remember testosterone which was subsequently lacking in your next choice.'

'Well, he'd just finished with me. Or at least we'd finished. He was going to America with his job and I didn't want to go. He didn't seem too upset when I refused.'

'Ah, the rebound syndrome?'

'Exactly. Austin said all the right things at just the right time. He was very charming. He could make me believe anything was possible, even if it wasn't.'

'My dear, he was a *politician.* That's what they do.'

'Yes, I realise that now but he was just on the edge of politics then. It became an obsession later – nothing else mattered. I put up with it though. The constant meetings, the dinner parties ruined through political differences, the losing of friends as they fled before they were cornered in an eternal hell of 'Politics Explained to the Lesser Mortal.' I put up with the phone calls interrupting our sacred time together; his late-night meetings that meant we hardly saw each other…'

'Well if you put up with it then – and more fool you- why are you here now?'

Sadie threw the rest of the wine down her throat and sat bolt upright.

'Because the telephone calls and late-night meetings were nothing to do with politics and everything to do with his secretary. The pathetic, nondescript, boring little sod had a mistress!'

There was a long pause where Em absentmindedly filled up Sadie's glass, which Sadie had absentmindedly held up to be filled.

'What I can't understand love, is why you think that's a loss?'

Sadie snatched her glass away in anger (being very careful not to spill any) and drew herself up to her full sitting-down height. 'I loved him.'

'Did you? smiled Em enigmatically, 'Did you really?'

Sadie suddenly felt very sober. She was thinking clearly, which was probably an illusion as everyone thinks that when they've had too much to drink.

'I thought I did.' she managed lamely.

'And now? How do you feel about him now? Angry or betrayed? Grief-stricken or relieved?'

Sadie tried to focus on her aunt who she thought looked suspiciously calm and collected for someone who had drunk a bottle of wine and then found some sherry at the back of a cupboard. She thought about the question, then sighed, then thought again.

'Okay, I suppose I'm relieved.'

'Hurrah!' shouted Em, who got up and did a little Egyptian-style dance around the settee, which dispelled any thoughts Sadie had of her still being sober.

'But that was five years dedicated to someone who didn't deserve it. Giving up managing the art gallery to be his campaign manager. That was my *life* Em.' she slurred

14

'Aren't you glad it isn't now?' said Em, sitting down and looking straight into her eyes.

On reflection, Sadie thought, closing her eyes to concentrate better, she *was* glad it wasn't her life now. Even though she had no idea what her life now was going to be, she was sure it wasn't going to involve policies, elections, delegates, campaigns, budget deficits or constituents ever again.

'Ah, bliss', she mumbled and then promptly fell asleep, her half-full glass held erect like a shining beacon of hope – with not a drop spilled.

Chapter 3

The sun shone relentlessly through the bedroom window and even though Sadie had pulled a pillow over her head, she could still feel the rays seeping through.

'Rain would be good' she mumbled. To suit her mood and in deference to her thumping head.

After another five minutes of the sun doing its Mr Happy impressions, Sadie took the hint and swung her legs out of bed. Viewed through slitty eyes functioning under a wine-induced headache, she noticed that her old room was just the same. Very 'Country Diary of an Edwardian Lady' with its pastel-coloured flowers on a pale ochre background. She turned her head slowly to the side and saw the quilt that used to be Em's when she was younger, all floral pale greens and yellows. She smiled and was glad Em hadn't tried to change anything.

Her eyes adjusted further afield after a few blinks to focus and alighted on a figure of Gaea, Mother Goddess of the Earth, which her aunt had sculpted for her tenth birthday, just over two decades ago. Sadie had found a book containing the illustration on Em's bookshelves -one of her grandfather's old books - and loved it. Em had taken a look and told her she thought it was Gaea because of the flowers in her hair. The next time she came, the statue was there, in her bedroom. Sadie hadn't wanted to take it home with her to the sterile, sharp-edged house she shared with her parents. It belonged here, amongst the flowers and nature it represented and superstitiously, she used to think that it would always bring her back here, where she belonged.

Looking out of the window, she could see the church. Em's cottage was called Church View but nearly all the houses in the village had at least a partial view of the church with it being built on a hill.

The smell of burnt toast, a testament to her aunt's limited cooking skills, greeted her as she entered the kitchen.

'Morning love' trilled Em, a little too loud, 'stuff in the fridge for breakfast- and by the look of you, you need plenty of carbs. You know where your key is? I'm off to the yard to collect more stone for a new commission. You look like death.'

'Thanks'

'Just saying. A walk across the moors? Up the lane to the wood? Into the village'

'A walk anywhere at the moment is not uppermost in my mind' her niece groaned.

'Best thing for a hangover. FRESH AIR!' she shouted in capital letters, then Em was off through the door and throwing herself into the battered land rover she'd had for years, spraying up odd bits of gravel and dust as she went.

'How come *you* haven't got a hangover?' she semi-shouted after her but she knew 'years of practice' would have been the answer.

After scrutinising the fridge contents and realising she was hungry after all- she settled on melted cheese on toast, her ultimate hangover cure. A few minutes later her mobile rang and after precious seconds locating where the sound came from, then tipping out the contents of her voluminous handbag to get it, she saw it was Ali. She pressed the button.

'Hmmgff' she managed.

'You've arrived then? Thanks for letting me know. You could have driven into oblivion as far as I knew, your heart breaking over your beloved.'

'Stop talking total crap Ali – and please, keep your voice down'. Her best friend had a dark sense of humour.

'A thick head is it? I remember your Aunt Em when we stayed overnight on the way to Edinburgh. I lost 24 hours of my life.'

'To be fair' I grunted, 'I think I drank more than her.'

'Impossible'

'As much anyway. I think I needed to. God knows what I told her but I think Austin the Perfect Politician is in black-er books with her than he ever was before.'

'We all kept telling you but you wouldn't listen'

'Okay, can you let me off at an early station on the guilt trip until I've recovered please?'

Ali laughed and then went serious, very un-Ali-like.

'You sure you're okay? I know you don't show it but…'

'I promise you' she interrupted, At least I will be when I get some of Em's 'fresh air' torture'

'Sounds right. Listen, I'm travelling up to Harrogate in a few days' time. Can I pop in and see you? Not much of a detour.'

'Ali, I'd love that. Why don't you stay overnight? You can have my bed and I'll sleep on the sofa. Em won't mind- or even notice.'

'That sounds great'. Over the phone, there was a shout and a bang in the background. 'The boys are having a meltdown-and that includes George. Be in touch' and she hurriedly cut the conversation off.

Sadie smiled. Alice Calvert had been the only person she could relate to in the competitive circles to which she had belonged. The Politerati had proliferated and when you could see both sides, like Sadie, it was hard to get involved in all the backbiting and double-dealing. The 'I think you'll find I'm right' and the 'How can you possibly believe that?' aggression that regularly made up the larger portion of any meetings, dinners or parties involving Austin. Ali had been different.

'Bunch of tossers aren't they?' were her first words to Sadie 'All of them, especially your boyfriend.'

Sadie had wanted to take umbrage at this but found herself bursting out laughing and agreeing with her.

'What about your husband though, is he included?' Sadie had replied, looking over to the quiet man in the corner with a resigned smile on his face.

'George? God no, he hates them all. He's just learnt to be two-faced and get away with it. Could have been the perfect politician when you think of it – but unfortunately, he has a conscience, which counts him out of the running.'

George wasn't really two-faced. He was one of the nice guys, a doctor, who could manage to disagree with someone in such a pleasant way that they didn't realise he had done.

Chalk and cheese as a couple with two boisterous but lovable young boys, they had been the only thing keeping Sadie going at times. She was looking forward to seeing her friend again. Meanwhile, there was the dreaded fresh air to be tackled. Reluctantly, Sadie pulled on her trainers, holding on to the wall very carefully as she straightened up – head swimming- and opened the front door.

Immediately there was a frantic barking. The last person left in the house was going out and leaving the beigey mop alone. No way, thought Whisky. He barked again, looking meaningfully up at his lead, which was slung over the coat hook in the hallway.

'Okay, okay' groaned Sadie 'anything as long as you stop barking' and she reached up for the lead. Sensitive Sadie and Smug Whisky then stepped into the 'magic' fresh air, at least one of them wincing as they did so.

Chapter 4

As Sadie reached the outskirts of the village, her head stopped thumping and she held herself upright instead of hunched over in protective mode. She took in lungfuls of air, which wasn't particularly fresh but warm and still. She turned off into the lane, which led to the woods and saw a heat haze shimmering on the lane's surface ahead of her. She slowed her pace a little in the face of the sun for which her canine companion looked very grateful. Didn't she realise he had a fur coat on, he thought in doggie thoughts.

Sadie remembered Mab's Wood very well from her childhood. When she was 'shooed' out of Em's door so that her aunt could work in the studio, she tasted the glorious freedom which had been totally lacking in Selford, where she lived with her parents. Even at that age, she couldn't believe that her mother and aunt were sisters as they were so very different. Em said then that, in the absence of a gooseberry bush and a stork- a one-eyed crow had left her sister Andrea under a hedge of under-ripe brambles. She got scratched when her parents pulled her out, which accounted for the prickliness and sourness, which became her character. As Sadie was only six at the time, she believed this throwaway line from a distracted Em and later confronted her mother, wanting to know if she had felt cold under the brambles as her birthday was in February. The resulting 'discussion' over the phone was very heated – at least on her mother's side as she was sure she could hear her aunt laughing down the phone. Em did apologise to Sadie the next time and said it was just a silly story – but somehow it had seemed more real than believing her mother and Em were sisters. Looking back, somewhere between the two of them would have been a better role model.

She had joined up with some of the other village children of all ages who roamed the countryside during the holidays and they all disappeared for the day. Dens had been made between, underneath and even inside trees. On one memorable occasion, they had tried to break the village record for how many children could fit inside the hollow at the bottom of the biggest tree until one of the younger ones shoved at the back, started screaming to be let out as he had apparently just discovered what claustrophobia was.

Where were they all now? Belle, the girl with the runny nose, Patrick, her first crush, Thomas the studious one, Anne, the girl who had her hair cut like a pudding basin? Mostly moved away unfortunately as there was no work in a small village so they had either de-camped to the nearest large town of Gressleigh or even further afield.

She was approaching Whisky's usual stopping-off spot, some abandoned barns to the right of the lane. The little dog had always liked to sniff to see which of his friends had been there before him and then add his mark to the nearest corner.

As she waited for Whisky's serious sniffing to end, she looked at the barns as though for the first time. She wasn't sure how safe they were as the village children had been warned off the place - and so, of course, had maintained a mythical reputation in their eyes. Witches?

Dragons? - but it was possible that unsafe buildings might have been behind the warnings.

An ancient wooden gate and an overgrown grass driveway led from the right of the barns and because Sadie could see some sort of courtyard appearing tantalisingly close by, she suddenly decided she would like to defy all the earlier warnings and have a good nose around.

She thought of climbing over the gate as it wouldn't budge but it looked too rickety. Besides, Whisky would never manage the acrobatics. Whisky immediately solved that problem by squeezing through the bars of the gate and running off, lead trailing behind him. Sadie realised if she lifted the gate up a few inches, the catch would work. Carefully reversing the process to shut it behind her she called the little rascal's name. She had wanted to see the barn but on reflection, it wasn't really a good idea trespassing on other people's property.

Walking round the corner of the barn she could see there were three sides bordering the courtyard, with multiple doorways, all perfect for a small dog to enter and hide. She glanced in all of them quickly and registered some sort of stables or workshops, small, stone-walled rooms but all empty with no sign of Whisky.

She ran carefully across the cobbles and out onto the driveway, calling the dog's name with a note of panic now. Returning to the gate, she looked up and down the lane with no canine sign, then made her way up the driveway and past the barns.

About a hundred yards further on, she glimpsed a building through the trees to her left and heard a familiar, yappy bark.

'Whisky!' she shouted and carried on, trying to find a break in the trees where she could climb through. Ahead though, the driveway curved to the left and she found herself in the open. There was a large, stone cottage there, which looked like it had once been whitewashed but very little of the wash now remained. It didn't look in bad condition but it had a definite air of neglect. It didn't feel to Sadie that anyone was living there. It gave off an abandoned air whilst still retaining the feeling that the house had once been loved. She knocked gingerly on the solid front door, not wanting to wander about the grounds dog-hunting, in case the owners came out with a shotgun. No answer, so she risked a peep through the window. An empty, unlived-in room. At least she could search with a clear conscience.

Suddenly there was a yap and the delinquent dog stood behind her, wondering what all the fuss was about.

'You little terror!' gasped Sadie.

Terrier, please! thought Whisky

'Don't you do that again! Come here right away' and she grabbed the lead and hugged a very confused Whisky. 'Let's go home now'.

Sadie was in desperate need of a cup of tea and the wood could wait till tomorrow. With her back to the house, she surveyed the garden. A large grass area, as broad as it was long, wasn't too overgrown, suggesting that someone must be cutting it periodically. Why would they, puzzled Sadie, when the house was obviously unlived-in? There were deep flowerbeds bordering the grass at each side and, unbelievably, some tall cottage garden plants were pushing their way through the general chaos.

She was standing on a small terrace, grass growing through the cracks, which had a set of three steps going down to the grass, with a low stone wall at either side of them. There were a couple of empty urns used as planters there on the terrace at the top of the steps.

The whole place had an abandoned 'Marie Celeste' air about it. Although it was strange it seemed to Sadie to have a friendly feel about it, despite outer appearances. As though it had been a happy home at some time and still gave off that aura. Shaking her head slightly to dispel the unbidden thoughts, it only served to remind her that the self-inflicted headache was still there, waiting to resurface. She set off back down the driveway with Whisky firmly held on his lead.

As she closed the gate behind her with difficulty, she looked for the house but could see nothing. The trees in the driveway and at the border with the lane hid the old cottage entirely. A secret cottage! She wondered if her aunt knew anything about it. Keeping tight hold of the lead, she walked back down to the village where a kettle, a cup of tea and more carbohydrates awaited her.

Chapter 5

Sitting at the kitchen table eating a supper of vegetable pasta, Sadie glanced at her harassed-looking aunt who had hardly said a word since she had emerged late from her studio.

'Everything going okay?' she ventured. This seemed to open the floodgates as Em sighed, plonked her fork down and held forth.

'That workshop is just too dark and poky, North facing. It's never been ideal but it's all I've got' Then she shook her head determinedly, 'No, it's not even that. I just can't get it right. Bloody fairy clinging on to a tree trunk, who the hell would want that?'

Sadie supposed it was a commission she was working on– and a fairy/tree combination sounded lovely to her. It reminded her of Mab's Wood.

'I have to say that the idea sounds good, why don't you like it?'

'It just', another sigh, 'isn't flowing. The fairy is too chunky. You don't get chunky fairies.'

'Couldn't you just...pare her down a little?' offered Sadie with some trepidation.

'You don't understand, it's not the width of her, it's the *essence* of her.'

Em was right, she didn't really understand, although perhaps... Something was forming in her mind.

'You mean she's too substantial?'

Em leapt on the idea. 'Too substantial! You've got it. What was it that Shakespeare said? "All this is but a dream, too flattering sweet to be substantial". My fairy is not a sweet dream, she is a Fat Fairy.'

Sadie smiled, she had seen Em despondent before – it didn't usually last long.

'I meant to ask you when I saw you...'

'Sorry, I got caught up with that damn design.'

'...about the barns on the Mab's Wood lane going out of Brytherstone. There's like a little courtyard arrangement.'

'Mmm' mumbled Em, lost in thoughts of overweight fairies.

'*And*' she continued, purposely omitted the dog-running-away incident, 'there was an abandoned cottage up the driveway next to it, with a fantastic garden. It looked empty – does anybody live there?'

Em's eyes slowly came back into focus and she leaned forward with interest.

'Acorn Cottage,' she smiled, 'the ancestral home. What did you think?'

Sadie was just about to mention that she had looked through the window, when she registered what Em had said.

'Ancestral home? It surely doesn't belong to you?'

Em laughed in an ironic 'I wish' sort of way.

'Unfortunately, no. It was owned by your great-grandmother though. Your great-grandfather was killed just before the end of World War II. Your grandad was only three years old and she brought him up in that cottage. He lived there till he went to work for the Winterhill Estate and lived in this cottage, which was tied to the estate then. When he got married to my mum, they allowed mum and dad to buy it from them at a ridiculously low price– and here I still am.'

'I wish I'd met them, my Grandad and Grannie, I mean'

'You'd have loved them. Dad kept going up to take care of his mother, maintaining the cottage; he was a carpenter/handyman. Towards the end, she stayed in most of the time, getting Mum or Dad to do her shopping and only venturing out into the garden. Of course, people started calling *her* a witch then too.'

There was a moment's pause while again Sadie registered what had been said, then she sat up and fired questions at her aunt.

'A witch? My great-grandmother? Your grandmother? A WITCH? ' Another pause, 'and what do you mean 'too'? You never told me about this!'

Em pushed her half-finished supper away and grabbed a bottle of red from the worktop.

'We might need this; it looks like it's going to be a long night.

*

Sadie sat on the bench in the small back garden and hugged her knees to her chest. A steaming cup of coffee sat on the rickety bamboo table next to her and morning shafts of shimmering sun were breaking through. It was going to be a hot day.

She was lost in thought at the conversation she'd had with Em last night. Her aunt had apologised for not telling her sooner because it just hadn't occurred to her, which was about right for her mind-in-the-clouds aunt. It seemed strange that her mother had never told her of any of the family history, although on reflection, she doubted it would have interested her. She had even cut herself off from her own sister, Emma, only keeping the relationship going by sending her daughter packing to stay with her every summer. Family obviously wasn't important to Andrea Barnes. Luckily Em had said last night that she really looked forward to her niece's visits and always enjoyed her company too, 'which was more than she could say of her sister's', she couldn't help adding. Sadie's parents now lived in New York after a business venture lured them there. The place was just right for them. Busy, busy, busy. Sadie visited once every couple of years, whether she wanted to or not.

However, her ancestors hadn't wanted to move any further than this small village. In this fast-moving world, it was something that Sadie could relate to. She had always felt like she needed roots. Somewhere that belonged to her, a place, a little part of the country, a home. This village was as near as she had ever got to that, a feeling she was coming home every summer instead of being sent away from home. She thought it was all due to Em but now, perhaps it went deeper than that?

Acorn Cottage had started as a small thatched cottage. Then it had been extended at the back to provide a farmhouse to a working farm but had retained the Acorn Cottage name. Her family had owned it at least since the 1600s but very probably before that, although there were no deeds in existence to prove it. Her great-grandmother hadn't really been a witch, of course, just an old woman, ill in her last years. A few of the village children had whispered but it was just a childish game. It was a tradition, apparently, that Acorn Cottage was known locally as The Witch's House. It didn't seem to be meant in a nasty way as the Norwood family were well regarded in the village. True Brytherstone people.

Generations before, the ancestor who had been living in the cottage with her daughter in the 1600s had acquired a reputation – although she was really only a herbalist. Agnes Norwood had been dragged before a hastily arranged court to answer allegations of 'communing with the devil'; in bringing a village youth 'back from the dead'. Thankfully, the youth's father, Sir James Fitzherbert, spoke up for her and as he was the local Lord of the Manor, she was allowed her freedom.

Her daughter, Anne and Agnes herself still practised herbalism until the daughter took up with the boy they had cured, now a man the same age as Anne. He was the fourth son of Fitzherbert and so wasn't needed for the Estate, the Army or Church, so when Agnes died, John Fitzherbert moved into the cottage with Anne and together, they built the farm up into a well-run and profitable business. It continued until Sadie's great-grandfather went to war and was killed, and his wife gave up on the farm and sold most of the land off.

The cottage had been left to Andrea and Em's father who was three when his father had died. He had never known him but was close to his mother, taking over her affairs and taking good care of her. She was quite happy, pottering in the garden, knitting and reading books, looking forward to her son's visits but preferring to live a solitary life in her beloved cottage. When she died Sadie's grandfather hadn't wanted to take the place on, being estate manager at the local manor. He had a more than generous weekly pay packet and he was happy in this little cottage with his family. The cottage was a bit of a millstone around his neck. He sold it to a property developer (Sadie had winced at this), who wanted to build new houses there, which were desperately needed after the war. There was some difficulty, perhaps something in the deeds, a covenant, but the houses had never been built. Em couldn't remember what the reason was as she had been too young to be told – or even be interested. As far as she knew, the cottage still belonged to this man or his family business.

Sadie had never had 'family' before. A place in the history of that family and a place where she felt she belonged. She had always felt this of Brytherstone but thought it was because Em lived here but perhaps it was something more than that, something that reached down the years into her soul.

The Norwood name had carried down through all those years until the present day. Acorn Cottage had an important place in that history. Sitting there, sipping her now nearly cold cup of coffee, Sadie started thinking.

Chapter 6

It was Friday and Sadie's first week had almost passed. She felt a twinge in her gut when she thought of going back to London. It wasn't the fact that there was no longer anything there for her but because it meant leaving this place. She knew her old flat, the one she had before moving in and buying a place with Austin, would be ready for her. The tenants she had rented it to had been given notice and she felt bad for them but now their shared home was being sold, she had no choice. She couldn't have lived at the house anyway as Austin was still in residence until he and his 'beloved' found somewhere new. It wasn't that she'd agreed to this state of affairs; it was more like she had just wanted to get away from it all and go towards a place that meant peace to her – Brytherstone.

It had been raining for the last couple of days with an unseasonal, gusty wind blowing through the village and its valley. Now though, as she pressed her nose against the bedroom window, the sun reflected on the wet rickety roofs of the houses over the road and the village was bathed in a mellow glow. She could almost smell the freshness, which only comes with the warmth of the sun after rainstorms.

'Buttered, wholemeal rolls straight from the oven, with fresh home-made marmalade. So get your backside down here *now*!'

'Coming' Sadie laughed as she recognised Meg's voice. Meg was Em's oldest friend and they had grown up together in this village. Meg's husband had died about six months ago, so she spent even more time here with Em than she had before. Her baking, thought Sadie, sniffing the newly-baked bread, was legendary.

Mmm – lovely 'she said, taking a huge bite of a roll, piled with proper butter and just this side of too-sweet marmalade.

Meg looked as pleased as Punch and went back to helping Em to wash up.

'What are you up to today Sadie' asked Em, turning round to her, tea towel in hand which made her look unusually domesticated.

'I thought I might take the furry one for a walk to get rid of some of that energy. I didn't realise dogs could sulk that much.'

Whisky had made pointed trips to the front door and back many times with a martyred expression, as the furthest he'd been in the constant rain was to the newsagents just down the road. Unless you count being let out into the small garden, which Whisky obviously didn't.

'Great, that's you two sorted. I'm driving Meg into Gressleigh to look at flats.' and she exchanged glances with Meg, who heaved a theatrical sigh. Her rosy, chubby face took on an unaccustomed sadness and she absentmindedly pushed a grey hair away that had escaped from the unruly pile on top of her head.

Meg's husband, whom she adored, had left her in a precarious financial position after some ill-advised investments. So much so that she couldn't afford to keep on the Baker's Shop and the accommodation over it, although it was far too large for her and there was less than a year left of the lease anyway. She couldn't afford the new lease, put up out of reach, it was widely suspected, because the owners wanted the whole premises to turn it into a large Outdoor Shop full of hiking clothes and equipment. Meg had to admit it would do well round Brytherstone, which was a walker's paradise, but what would the village do without a bakery? There had been an outcry at first but now the shop was closed, everyone had settled to getting their loaves and cakes, bland as they were, from the small supermarket. At the end of this month, Meg would be homeless. There were small places she could afford in town but she wanted to stay in the village. Unfortunately, nothing was available.

Sadie gulped the last of her tea down then grabbed the lead, trying, with difficulty, to put it on an ecstatic, hairy pogo-stick. At the door, she turned back.

'Em, you haven't forgotten Ali's staying overnight, have you? She'll be here later today?'

Em rolled her eyes and tutted. 'Haven't forgotten. Not senile yet. She's not veggie now or anything is she?'

'Erm…' winced Sadie, remembering that she was indeed veggie,

Em sighed, 'I'll get some stuff from the deli'

Sadie shouted back her thanks as Whisky dragged her out onto the sun-bathed street.

There was a short pause inside the cottage.

'You'd forgotten about Ali hadn't you' said Meg quietly.

'Yep' replied Em.

'Good recovery' grinned Meg.

*

This time, Sadie was going to have a good look at Acorn Cottage. It may not be hers legally but it was historically. At least that would be her excuse if she met the owner up there.

Less than a mile outside the village she found herself near the barns again. Now, she knew how to open the gate and being careful to close it behind her, she made her way up the tree-lined drive. The branches were hanging low and Sadie had to duck more than once to avoid a tree branch between the eyes.

She experienced a thrill at seeing the cottage again. She had actually felt something like excitement or anticipation when she had first seen it and which now had determination added to it. She wanted to get inside, if at all possible, to see where her ancestors had lived and to see if she could feel anything of their presence there.

She knew it might be a hard-hat job, with crumbling plaster and wood-wormed staircases and maybe some dry rot or damp thrown in for good measure. She was also aware, although this was conveniently shoved to the back of her mind for now, that she was about to do some illegal breaking and entering. She just really felt this need to see if there was anything of her family's personality left in the house.

Sadie knocked loudly on the door – just in case- and waited a couple of minutes before she tried to open it. Locked of course. She looked through both front windows, which were ingrained with dirt. There was no remaining furniture that she could see. It would have been emptied ready for demolition before the owner's plans went wrong. She retraced her steps and then went round the side to the back of the house. The house walls went back further than the frontage suggested yet even the extensions at the back were very old.

As she rounded the corner, she gave an involuntary gasp. What a view! She walked out of the shade of the trees and looked down the long back garden where she could see a whole vista unfolding in front of her.

There was a wide stone terrace all along the back with a low balustrade surrounding it with three steps down, echoing the front terrace. Below that was a lawned area then further down and set to the right was what looked like a network of paths in a regular pattern with small overgrown patches between them. A potager or a herb garden? A continuation of Agnes's healing garden perhaps? After this, the land opened out onto a large and long grassy area and beyond, a patchwork of fields that went on for miles, as far as the eye could see.

The farmland undulated, dipping down tantalisingly, then rising at the other side, bearing different crops, now mustard yellow, now fresh green. The cornfields glowed in the sun and the barley rippled like a wind-blown sea. There were copses of leafy green trees dotted about and what looked like farmhouses, eventually reduced to doll's houses by distance. At the end of the vista, too far for the eye to make out well, rose some hills of misty, muted blues.

Sadie realised she had been holding her breath and blew it out in disbelief. The inside of her brain was bubbling with excitement as she made her way slowly through the garden. She walked over the large grassed area towards the end, which fell away a little, culminating in a ha-ha, a wide, deep ditch which kept the cows and sheep from the fields away from the garden. To each side, there were small trees, which on closer inspection, she could see were apple trees. As she turned and looked back, she could see that fruit trees had been planted all along the perimeter at each side, like a linear orchard. She saw, at the other side of the house, her right as she looked at it now, was what looked like a giant oak and she wondered if that was the same one that gave the cottage its name. She wasn't sure it could be that old?

Sadie found herself smiling involuntarily; it was all so perfect! If she could have described her dream property, this would have been it. Possibly not the property interior though as that was probably more of a nightmare. If she could just peep in the back windows, she might gain a better idea. She walked up to the back terrace again.

The large French window had thick, faded curtains drawn across it so no chance to be nosy there but there was a wide window a few feet away, which had a drainpipe with a drain below it. Probably the kitchen? The glass was so dirty though, it was impossible to make out anything other than vague shapes.

Rounding the other side of the cottage to the right, she again revelled in the glorious view there too. There was a large field, which she could remember cows grazing in when she was younger and then the land sloped very gently downwards towards Mab's Wood, not far away at all. There was a round building on this land at the other side of the oak, which looked rather like a stunted, disused windmill. Turning back to the cottage she saw another smaller window next to a large door at the side. She took hold of the doorknob while she peered in and gave it an experimental twist. It opened with a creak and as she pushed it open, she felt something behind the door – thoughts of dead bodies, rats rather than humans, made her shudder. The whole place will have been trashed, she thought, then realised this was Brytherstone and not London. She slowly crept in and then came to a standstill.

There was an old butler's sink, filthy and cobwebbed but unbroken. There was an old range that would have been black-leaded religiously but now lay under years of grime. It was set inside a large, sooty inglenook fireplace with a bread oven with no door. What looked like a huge pantry was at the far end of the room behind a half-open door. There were old, built-in wooden cupboards and in the centre, an old, rectangular, solid wooden table. There was a vast amount of space there and Sadie could see that, when all the windows were cleaned, the kitchen would be lovely and light.

She tiptoed into the hallway, afraid of waking the ghosts of the past who might not want their peace disturbed. They would be ghosts of *my* ancestors though, she thought, *my* family – so surely they wouldn't mind?

The floorboards were under a thick layer of dust but apart from that they looked to be in good condition. The floorboards continued into a room that Sadie recognised as the front room with the high and wide windows. The generous proportions, not apparent from the outside, were definitely more farmhouse than cottage although this was probably kitchen and living room combined originally. She caught sight of a window seat, made possible by the incredibly thick walls and hurried across. She had always loved the idea of having a window seat with a curtain across it that she could pull it behind her and hide – a throwback to reading Jane Eyre when she was young. Somewhere she could sit and read and gaze out of the window and dream of dashing heroes coming to rescue her.

Something caught her eye, or someone. A dark-haired man standing facing the house and for a moment she was confused as to which Bronte book this as the hero looked more Heathcliff-like. Then she felt a thud in her

stomach as she realised the man was all too real
and at this moment was striding purposefully
across the grass towards the cottage. Sadie gave
a tiny squeal like a child caught with her hand in
a jar of sweets. She flew back into the kitchen,
out of the kitchen door and round onto the rear
terrace. She had just decided to hide behind the
trees until she could make her escape when she
heard barking. Two lots of barking. One yappy,
one deeper. In unison.

Whisky! She had been so intent on her
discoveries that she had almost forgotten him,
despite the lead still wrapped over her hand. He
had been quietly sniffing round the garden with
her but had disappeared when she went into the
house. So much for hiding. She guiltily walked
round to the front of the house, calling Whisky's
name to show willing. Arriving there, she saw
there was a stand-off between the small Cairn
terrier and a larger border collie. She started to
run in case Whisky got attacked, although he
seemed to be holding his own very well.

'What the hell are you doing on this
property?' a deep voice called out to her
arrogantly and she saw the man had reappeared
from the other side of the house. He looked
pretty peed off with playing hide and seek. He

was dark-haired, the style longer than was fashionable. His eyes were narrowed but she could see they were glinting ice-blue below dark, lowered brows. He reached her and she noticed that he towered over her. She felt intimidated so hit back in defence.

'What are YOU doing here? I was told it was empty and had been for years.'

'I'm here to cut the fruit trees back'. He indicated the long pruners resting on his shoulder as though she was an idiot not to have noticed them before. Which she was. 'Now, what's *your* excuse?'

His attitude was still aggressive and demanding and it made Sadie's hackles rise. She didn't know where it came from but she drew herself to her full height, tilted her chin imperiously and said,

'I am a Norwood!'

It was as if a blade of steel had cut through the air between them. Sadie stopped breathing for a few seconds as she noticed the man's eyes widen and his lips part with astonishment. Nobody spoke as they stared at each other and the silence was intense. Sadie wavered a little, already regretting her outburst. The man seemed to shake his head a little and then cleared his throat.

'Norwood…?'

'Well, not exactly' she swallowed, backpedalling, 'I'm Sadie Barnes but my mother was a Norwood before she married and my Aunt Em, in the village, she still is a Norwood.'

'Em? Well if you are a Norwood' and he looked doubtful about that, 'then you have more right here than I do but if there's a next time, make sure you keep your fluffy toy on a lead' and with that, he turned on his heel and disappeared round the side of the building.

Who the hell did he think he was? Sadie bent to put the lead on Whisky who was yapping again with a new bravado now the other dog had gone. Admittedly, the border collie had looked more affronted than aggressive, unlike its master. It had sat at his feet, panting, while Whisky growled and yapped in confrontation, with little legs askance. How dare he tell her what to do on her own property? And here she brought herself up short. She was actually beginning to think of it as her property through heredity, whereas the disagreeable specimen with the pruners probably had more right to be here. Was he the owner? Probably not- just a maintenance man hired to keep up with the garden so it didn't get too overgrown. He was more likely just a gardener as the house didn't show any signs of maintenance.

She dragged a reluctant Whisky away because the little dog had obviously enjoyed the battle – or more likely, the huge grounds to run full pelt in. For the first five minutes, Sadie fumed inwardly at the man's attitude. The last time she'd felt like this was when she'd been told off by Mr . Gruesome Grant in front of the whole class for being one minute late. She had to admit technically, if not morally, she was in the wrong. Then and now.

Slowly, her thoughts turned to a small grain of an idea that had appeared from nowhere and by the time she had entered the village, it had taken root.

Chapter 7

Sadie clattered through into her aunt's workshop with a tray containing cheese and cucumber sandwiches and a mug of tea. She knew Em would forget to eat otherwise. Em, who had abandoned the Fat Fairy for now was sketching designs at her 'desk', a plaster and paint-splattered old table in the corner. Sadie then returned to the kitchen and spent most of the afternoon making phone calls and sending emails. At last, she put the phone down decisively and stretched her arms above her head to relieve the tension. Mid-stretch she croaked 'Ali!'

Quickly she jumped in the shower and put her hair up – no time to wash it. She put on a pair of white, skinny capri pants with a pastel pink blouse then hurriedly put on her mascara and a touch of lipstick just in time for the knock at the door.

'Sadie!' yelled Ali as the door opened to reveal a small elf-like woman with crazy blonde hair framing her face.

'Ali!' laughed Sadie and they hugged like they hadn't seen each other for months instead of weeks.

They had coffee after Ali had lost the argument of 'who gets the sofa' as Sadie wanted her to enjoy the peace of her bedroom as that peace was sorely lacking at home with her boys.

'Meg's coming to cook for us tonight; I hope you don't mind her staying for dinner?'

'Brilliant!' said Ali, 'I certainly don't mind if she's cooking us a meal. Her baking is delicious, especially those cheese scones. Mmm…' she went off into daydreams about food.

'Before that though, I need to take you to the pub for a private word' said Sadie.

'Ooh, sounds ominous. About what?'

'Can't tell you here'

'What's with all the Secret Squirrel malarkey?

Sadie moved her head closer and whispered, just in case,   'There's something I need to discuss with you but I don't want Em to know yet. So I'd be grateful if you didn't mention it to her when you see her. If it starts to become solid, instead of just an idea, then I'll tell her straight away.'

'Okay but what makes you think I can help you?'

'You'll see' said Sadie enigmatically as she dragged her friend out to the Falling Stone Inn at the other end of the village.

*

Settled in a quiet corner with a gin and tonic, Ali wiggled her eyebrows and leaned forward conspiratorially, looking furtively around her.

'Listen vairy carefully, I vill say zis only once. The password is Supercalafragil…'

'Okay, okay' laughed Sadie, 'It's not really a secret. I just don't want to get Em's hopes up.'

'Come on then, what's the plan?'

'Well, you know my flat in London, the one I rented out when Austin and I bought the house together? '

Ali nodded.

'And you know you said your brother was looking to buy in that area as it's near his new job?'

Ali widened her eyes and nodded more slowly.

'Do you think he'd like to buy *my* flat from me? I can do him a good deal if I can get the money quickly. You said he'd moved out of his flat and was renting now, didn't you? '

'Yes, he has…er, is…' said Ali distractedly and then focussed on Sadie.

'Does that mean you're moving out of London then? I know you and ski-slope nose are selling the house you shared but I thought you'd be moving back to the flat?'

Sadie was worried she'd disappointed her friend and she wondered again about the reality of her idea.

'I was going to' she replied apologetically, 'I gave notice as soon as I found out about Austin, and the tenants are moving out next week. That's why I'm here in the first place – apart from it being my favourite 'get away from it all' place. In my mind, I always intended to move here at some point in the future but something has come up that may make moving here more urgent. I'm going to need both the money from my flat and the half share from my house if it's going to work.'

'If *what's* going to work?' Ali looked bewildered.

Sadie took a deep breath, 'I want to buy a house here, in Brytherstone. Not just any house but my old ancestral home- which is as much a surprise to me as it is to you.'

She laughed at Ali's expression. 'I know, it makes it sound like a stately home but it's just a cottage. An old farmhouse really, although there's no farmland as such now. All the agricultural fields have been sold off to surrounding farms. There's a courtyard of buildings down the drive that I sort of have plans for too, things are coming together in my mind but for now...'

Sadie stopped her stream-of-consciousness deluge as she noticed the astonished look on Ali's face.

'I'm just checking that you still have your faculties and it isn't the country air that's affected you...?

'I'll be honest, that's not the reaction I was hoping for Ali.' Sadie couldn't help feeling disappointed.

'What about a job? You were originally thinking about going back to your art gallery work?'

'If things work out, I will have a new and completely different job here' Sadie replied defensively.

'You're getting out of the rat race and away from the Mother Ship?' said Ali, whose eyes were like saucers now.

'Well, hopefully, yes' Sadie was now thoroughly crestfallen until she saw Ali's face widening into a huge incredulous grin, while she did a little victory dance in her seat at the same time.

'HURRAY! YES! SADIEEEEEE' yelled Ali as she reached across to envelop her in a bear hug and one old local who'd just come through the door hesitated as to whether he should go straight out again.

'I've been so worried about you' said Ali as she finally released her friend, 'you've been so down since the Austin incident that I didn't think I was going to see you this enthusiastic again – ever. I'm really pleased you've found something you're happy with in a place you love. Even if it does mean moving away from me.' Ali pretend-pouted.

Sadie couldn't hide her relief and she even more determined to go ahead with her plans now.

'Just make sure it's what you want before I ask my brother as I don't want to get his hopes up if you change your mind.'

'I'm 99% positive. I have chased things up and put certain guarantees in place. I think it's too late to change my mind now anyway. I will think of nothing else though until you return home from Harrogate and I've filled in the missing blanks, then I'll ring you to confirm. Is that okay? Whatever happens with Acorn Cottage though, I think my heart belongs to this place and I will move here anyway.'

To celebrate this about turn in Sadie's life, Ali went to the bar to order two more G&Ts. She waited while the lugubrious landlord adjusted the pumps, washed out a tray, had a conversation with the old man at the bar about a sick cow, straightened some beer mats and finally came to take her order.

'Now I know why it's called the Falling Stone. You stand so long waiting to be served that you turn to stone and fall over.' Ali offered.

Jez Cobb's mouth twitched at the corners but he just said,

'Been done that one girl, been done'

Ali grinned and winked at him as she ordered the   drinks.

Chapter 8

Em raced the land rover into Brytherstone at a rate that had Meg pushing imaginary brakes to the floor in the passenger seat. Pulling up outside her cottage, she disgorged Meg and the food supplies onto the pavement, along with the front door key. She then roared off again, leaving Meg blinking in a cloud of dust and shaking her head in recognition. Em was in one of *those* moods.

Em's foot gradually eased off the accelerator as she started to climb the hill leading out of the village towards Gressleigh again. This time though, she turned off onto a side lane, which bore the impressive National Trust sign 'Winterhill Manor'. She sighed and continued up the leafy lane.

She stopped at a gated entrance from which she could see a huge Jacobean building with a large knot garden leading down to a small, oval lake containing a marble fountain. A dusty white car park stood to her right. She ignored all this, driving to her left instead, down a driveway, which led to a lodge which was nearly as impressive as Winterhill Manor but on a much smaller scale. A gatehouse, ostensibly but rather a grand one, Winterhill Lodge was a gabled house with a portico. There was a lovely cottage garden spilling over with larkspur, lupins and foxgloves. It was picture-perfect but none of this mattered to Em at the moment.

She slammed the door of the 'jalopy' and strode to the door. She knocked but went in without waiting for an answer.

'Are you in?' she shouted

'No dear, I just leave the door unlocked in case any riff-raff want to help themselves to the family silver'

'I'm not in the mood'

'No, I can tell that.'

James Fitzherbert, otherwise known as James, Earl of Gressleigh, stuck his head warily around the kitchen door.

'Coffee? Or something stronger?' he asked.

'Something stronger. No – I'm driving, just stronger coffee.'

James made the coffee as Em sat with ants in her pants on the sofa, unable to calm down.

'Alright, what is it?' asked James, placing the steaming mug in front of her.

Em looked at him. He looked so tired nowadays. He had always had that blue-eyed, blond-haired youthfulness about him, inherited from his blue-blooded family. Now, since he'd handed over the Manor to the National Trust and moved to the Lodge, he'd had that defeated look about him. Restoration costs had spiralled and he couldn't keep up. Although finances should be easier now, he felt like he'd let generations of his family down. The Lodge was a grand residence that he should be proud of but he felt he would be known as the one who finally 'gave up'. Em calmed down a little and smiled at him.

'It's nothing really'

'Which is why you nearly decimated my delphiniums as you stormed in?'

'I didn't! Well, okay, I'm maybe a little hot and bothered.' she conceded as James waited patiently for an explanation, 'My commission for your lakeside statue is not going well. I think because it's not for you anymore but for the guardians of your house. I can't put as much into it. I can't *feel* it.'

'And if the National Trust had asked you to the same commission for another of their properties- how would you feel then?'

Em was silent for a moment.

'Better, I suppose'

'Then just get on with it Em, it's a work of art. Not for me, not for you but for the public who will admire this piece in these wonderful surroundings. We can admire it too just as much as we ever could. Don't you agree?'

Em slowly and reluctantly nodded.

'Then there's Meg.'

'Is she alright?' James looked worried as he knew what she'd been through recently.

'Of course she's not. She's lost her husband, been forced out of her home and livelihood, been forced to look for accommodation - because of financial constraints and availability - in a town when she's a country person- a Brytherstone person – through and through. Do you want more?'

'Not particularly' he raised an eyebrow and Em had the grace to look chastened. 'She's not found anywhere yet then?'

Em sighed. 'To be honest, there have been a few options but her heart isn't in it. Time is running out. Her heart belongs to the village but there just isn't anywhere for her.'

James looked at Em and smiled. She was taking on the problems of the world again. She could cope with everything that was thrown at her personally but when it came to her friends, she was like a tigress on their behalf. She was intensely loyal and James hoped she knew just how much he appreciated it, as he knew Meg did.

'I'm sure she'll find something Em. Trust in fate. Can't you cast a spell like your ancestors to make a Brytherstone property become available?'

Em threw her coaster at his head, which luckily missed and landed on the dog bed. Rupert, the aged red setter, looked up, blinked a few times and then went back to sleep.

'So, I have to go killing off village residents to get my friend a home do I? It can be arranged in her ex- landlord's case…' she sniffed.

James reached across and put his hand over hers.

'Look, she can always stay here until she finds somewhere; I've got two spare bedrooms.'

Em looked up at him and thought of two things at once. One, how kind this man had always been and two, why didn't she think of that? She scraped her chair back, making Rupert's eyes open at least a centimetre.

'Of course! She can stay with me until a place becomes available, or we kill each other, whichever comes first.'

'You know you've never argued. It's impossible to argue with Meg, it's like kicking a puppy.' James frowned. 'What about Sadie?' He had known her since she was young and was very fond of her.

'Oh,' murmured Em as though the thought hadn't occurred to her. 'I'm not turning Sadie out whatever happens – but she's only supposed to be staying for a couple of weeks until her flat's ready. Sadie is the priority though and if she wants to stay longer...'

Em looked thoughtful and James kept quiet. Best to let her just get on with it.

'I know!' shouted Em suddenly, 'there's the attic!' Then blowing James a kiss she left the lodge in much the same way as she entered. Like a tornado entering the house, doing a quick recce, and then leaving again.

James watched her drive off with a silly smile on his face. She drove him mad but he couldn't help it – he loved that woman.

Chapter 9

The dinner the previous evening had gone very well with Ali and Em exchanging banter while Meg and Sadie wiped tears of laughter away. Sadie hoped Ali would be getting in touch with her any time now. She had left another message on Ali's phone saying that she was 100 percent certain now that she wanted to go ahead with the sale, whatever happened with Acorn Cottage, she wanted to move back here to the village. There were still more arrangements to make though and questions to ask. She consulted another piece of paper and then punched the number in her phone.

'It's time you put that phone down and started to relax!' frowned Em, walking into the kitchen and catching her on the phone yet again.

Sadie mimed 'five minutes' and walked nonchalantly into the living room so that Em wouldn't hear. You couldn't get much past her aunt so she would have to start explaining soon. After a while, she bounced back into the kitchen.

'Any more of Meg's cheese scones left or has Ali eaten them all? she asked Em.

'She packed the rest up to take with her I think but Meg's coming round later to do some baking, with everything being packed away there, so if you ask her nicely…?'

'What's happening there?' Sadie frowned, 'When has she got to be out and where will she go?'

'She has to be out very soon and well…' there was an unusual hesitancy to Em's words 'I was thinking she could come here? She just about lives here anyway and she would be like a fish out of water in Gressleigh. I was wondering if you could spare the time to help me sort the attic out? It hasn't been used in years since it was my bedroom. Your mother demanded her own when she was twelve'

'That sounds like my mother.' Sadie agreed 'I didn't realise you slept up there though, I thought it had always been used for storage. I always thought it would be a great den, especially as it has 'proper' stairs to it, like a third floor rather than a tiny loft. I used to go up there sometimes and look out of that window; you could see more miles, right over the rooftops.'

'I loved it too for that reason and the fact that it was well away from your mother' Em grinned. 'Later I just bunged things up there that I didn't need and they've been there so long that I'm sure I never *will* need them now. I'll get rid of them – apart from the old family stuff of course.'

'I'll definitely help but please, let Meg have my old room, as long as I can take Gaea and my quilt,' she laughed 'I can use the attic for now as I'm not permanent and Meg will be.'

'We'll see' said Em reluctantly 'I always think of that as 'your' room – but it *is* one less flight of stairs for her. The attic could do with a clear-out anyway, there are long-lost things in that room. I think I left my sense of humour and my dignity up there years ago and haven't found them yet.'

'Your sense of humour has never left you Em' laughed Sadie 'Your dignity, however…'

She narrowly avoided a towel thrown at her head.

'Of course I'll help you clean out the attic, it should be interesting but first, I'm going to take Whisky for a walk'

'That animal is getting more exercise than he's ever had in his life. He's used to being idle and pampered- you'll wear him out!'

Sadie laughed and grabbed the lead and the yapping 'mop' before Em, who was looking suspicious, could ask any questions.

*

On reaching the courtyard at the end of the Acorn Cottage driveway, she had a serious word with Whisky, who wanted to escape and explore again. She had to keep him nearby as she didn't want anyone complaining about them, not at this stage.

Sadie dragged the sulking dog around the stalls, where he brightened up as it gave good sniffing options. Although when Sadie moved some old straw, which still contained 'organic matter', Whisky suddenly didn't seem too keen. The spaces looked like they may have been used for horses, rather than the cows she had been told were housed there. They were individual units – perhaps when the big horses had been kept, when they used to pull the ploughs in times gone by. More than one had been used as workshops judging by the hooks still in the walls and the remains of rotting shelves. She had a good look at the beams, walls, doors and floors. The floors were old flagstones, a little uneven in places. The roof, surprisingly, was only showing the sky through a little in two or three places but she supposed more tiles would want replacing than was at first obvious. The rest of it would need a deep clean and disinfecting but the stone walls looked in good repair – it was a solid building. If her plan was to work, each of these stalls, eight in total, could become an individual unit. They looked to be about 10x12 feet, apart from the one in the far right corner, which was a little bigger. She hoped, perhaps optimistically seeing them again, to rent each one out to an individual craftsman or woman and for the whole courtyard to become a creative Arts and Crafts centre.

She smiled to herself, thinking of Ali's remark about her newly-found enthusiasm. She *was* enthusiastic about this and she felt a new life being breathed into her, which was all tied up with this place – both Acorn Cottage and Brytherstone itself. Perhaps her aunt could use one, although these wouldn't be big enough for a new workshop, which was a shame as she desperately needed one. Meg could use one for her artisan pastries and cakes. She herself would like one but hadn't quite formulated what she could do with it yet.

The courtyard was about half a mile down a lane that led off from the main road to the village. Not an A road but busy enough to get plenty of passing trade. A sign just before turn-off would alert people. Up the driveway a little behind the courtyard, there was an overgrown area, which appeared to have cobbles underneath, the same as the courtyard. If the brambles and ivy were cleared, there was potential to make a small car park for perhaps ten or twelve cars. She went back to the driveway and looked up towards the cottage. A sign could be put there saying 'Private' because that would lead to her house, which would remain completely private anyway as it couldn't be seen through the barrier of trees. Sadie stopped making plans for a moment and reflected on what she had just thought. Her house. Oh, it sounded wonderful. She knew she shouldn't count her chickens before they were hatched but she was running on an adrenalin surge at the moment.

Now, thought Sadie, it was time to go and check 'her' house more thoroughly if possible before she got back to the solicitors. She bent down to Whisky, keeping tight hold of the lead.

'Best behaviour, remember.'

Chapter 10

The kitchen door was still unlocked. She had a perverse thought that she ought to secure it so people like her couldn't enter at will. Taking a sneaky look over her shoulder to make sure that the even grumpier version of Heathcliff wasn't lurking there again, she stepped into the kitchen. Going from room to room, she was pleasantly surprised as, if you discounted the thick layers of dust and cobwebs, it looked almost habitable. She went through each room on the ground floor: the huge kitchen; the only slightly smaller living room and what could have been a dining room opposite the kitchen. There was a much smaller room opposite the living room off the hallway, which she earmarked for her study. A cavernous broom cupboard lurked between the dining room and study, which she might possibly make into a downstairs cloakroom as the cupboard under the stairs was big enough for a hoover, ironing board etc. She didn't have a great deal of paraphernalia to bring. Possessions that were shared between her and Austin, she mostly didn't want anything to do with. There were a few things from the flat but that was all.

She was more nervous going upstairs as she had noticed a few slipped or missing tiles and was anticipating damp patches at the very least. Again, she was surprised at how solid it all seemed. Yes, there were a couple of damp patches but it was obvious where the damp was coming from and it could hopefully be put right. She earmarked the room above the living room for her bedroom as you could see right down the valley over the treetops. She was generally very pleased at the condition of the cottage. Whether a surveyor would agree with her, she was yet to find out.

Stepping out of the door and facing down over the back garden and the fields beyond, she carried on towards the bottom of the garden. She halted at the bottom end so she could just stare at the beautiful view - she didn't think she could ever tire of this. As she turned back, she caught sight of what looked like a shed through the trees bordering the garden to the left. Walking towards it, she realised there was a gap between the trees, a pathway, which led to a green and lush clearing. She walked through the gap and was brought up short, by what she had thought was a shed. She blinked her eyes in disbelief. It was a Gypsy caravan – vardo didn't they call this type? It seemed very old and definitely original. As she came closer, she could see that a lot of the ornate and latticed carving was broken off and it needed repainting, the gold scrolling had faded and what looked to have been bright colours were now washed out. The roof looked okay though and the steps leading up to the door hadn't rotted, although a couple of panes of glass had cracked. It seemed to have decayed at the same rate as the cottage. They built houses – and caravans – to last in those days obviously.

The windows were too high up at the side to look in and she discounted the steps as one of the wheels was listing, so she daren't climb up and be nosy. She would love to see inside though. Going round to the rear, there was a break in the trees to reveal a patchwork of fields and a big blue sky, the same view as she had from her garden.

This was fascinating! Why was it here? She made a mental note to ask Em if she knew anything about it and carried on exploring as she had seen a path starting at the other side of the clearing. The path was bordered to the left by small trees, (maybe crab apple?) - and to the right by the open land leading to a large wheat field. She had walked a hundred yards with Whisky straining at the leash now for his freedom. 'Not yet' said Sadie, wagging her finger in mock severity but as she looked in front of her, she could see what looked like the top part of Mab's Wood at the other end of the footpath. The wood created a ridge along the hill all the way back down to the road and Sadie could see it was spread out much wider at this end.

She couldn't remember coming up this far when she was a kid. Their childhood playground was much nearer to the road so they could make a quick getaway if the Spirit of Mab ever appeared. She laughed at the thought of their childish imaginations. There wouldn't be any harm in letting him have his freedom now so she released a very excited Whisky. She looked for a path that might lead her back to the road, through the wood but the trees were thicker at this end and she couldn't detect a path at all. Perhaps no one ever came this far. By staring closely at the ground she discovered a faint track through the grass, she followed it a little way before she realised there was no sign of Whisky.

Panicking and calling his name, Sadie stumbled along the path, which appeared to be leading her further into the wood, away from the lane she wanted to reach. She picked the pace up when she heard Whisky yapping furiously- and was that another lower bark too? Oh no, this couldn't be happening again, she thought.

Running now, Sadie came to a clearing where, to her surprise, a Scandinavian-style log cabin stood. A super deluxe one, almost like a grown-up tree house but on the ground! Santa's Lapland luxury cabin, here in Brytherstone. More frantic barking brought Sadie down from her flight of fancy and she raced round the cabin, to where the noise was coming from -and to confront her worst fears.

Here was the doggie stand-off again, between the Cairn Terrier in the left-hand corner of the ring and the Border Collie in the right. Seconds out – Round Two. There was a movement to her left and before she had time to register the collie's owner, his voice rang out,

'You again. What are you doing on my land?'

It took a minute to sink in but Sadie came back, guns blazing.

'Your land? This wood is a public right of way, always has been.'

'Not this part' he shot back 'This is my land, bought and paid for by my family from your family'

Sadie was taken aback. Mab's Wood belonged to her ancestors? Another thing she didn't know.

'Why did they sell it?' she managed to whisper.

'There was trust between them' he shook his head dismissively 'Too much to go into now – but they did. I have the documents inside'

Sadie was momentarily struck dumb so he pressed home his advantage.

'And now, if you wouldn't mind taking yourself and your aggressive mutt off my land…'

She stared at him. How could he be so rude? His eyes were like blue shards of glass glinting menacingly under jet-black brows. And dark eyelashes. Very dark and long eyelashes. His almost black hair falling across his forehead as he moved. He looked like a magnificent tall, broad-shouldered warrior defending his castle. She came back to earth and shook herself mentally, betrayed by her own thoughts and annoyed at the image she'd conjured up. She couldn't even think of any sarcastic retort to throw back at him. All she could manage was,

'There doesn't seem to be much trust between our families now, does there?' and she was rewarded by a momentary flicker of doubt in his eyes.

'Come on Whisky, let's go.' she said with as much dignity as she could muster and they both turned towards the dogs who were now suspiciously quiet.

To the obvious surprise of the human contingent, the dogs were now play-fighting and jumping around in glee, interspersed with much licking of each other's ears. Betrayed again thought Sadie, first by my thoughts and now by my dog. What was all that pretend aggression when they obviously liked each other? The dogs, she meant, of course, batting away another thought that occurred to her about that question. Unbelievable! With that, she clipped the little dog's lead on and dragged a reluctant Whisky away from his new playmate.

Chapter 11

By the time Sadie reached Em's cottage, her anger had been walked off and she could smile a little at the expression on the man's face when he realised his own dog had turned traitor. The terrier and the sheepdog had obviously decided to bury the hatchet and become friends, unlike their human owners.

There was no sign of Em in the kitchen or her studio so Sadie put the kettle on and went upstairs to fetch her notebook. Halfway up she heard bumps and moans from up above and for one heart-stopping moment thought of ghosts until she realised her aunt must have made a start on the attic room.

'Em' she shouted, 'do you need a hand? Or caffeine?'

'Both' came the decidedly grumpy reply.

Five minutes later, steaming coffees resting on a rickety wooden side table, they were both sitting on a threadbare rug and pulling boxes across to them.

'I wondered where that had got to' said Em in astonishment, 'I didn't realise it had been sent to Coventry up here.'

She held up a decidedly gaudy Chinese-looking vase.

'It's worth a lot of money this, I can sell it.'

'Not of sentimental value then?' replied Sadie with amusement.

'I think it was a wedding present for my parents. It was always on display when I was young as the friends who bought it still came round regularly but it was obviously banished when the friends moved. If I can't get money for it, it can be sent back to Coventry.''

Sadie unwrapped a statue from some old newspaper. It was of a couple dancing and when she was younger, she had always thought it must have been a model of her mum and dad.

'Can I have this in my room?' she asked, checking it for damage.

'Please – take anything you want. As Meg is now moving into your old room when you return to London, I don't have to clear this room yet but

I feel like I'm on a mission. Besides, when you come and stay again, which I hope will be soon, it will be your new bedroom in case Meg is still here'

'That's fine by me; I like it up here, once we get those nets from the gable window. How do you feel about Meg staying long term Em?'

'I don't mind how long she stays, I'm usually in the workshop anyway but Meg, despite being pretty mild-mannered, is quite independent and I'm sure she'd like her own place. As long as that place was in Brytherstone – and therein lies the problem.'

Another hour or so and they had made great inroads into the 'junk' and the floor was much clearer. They called it a day and Em was just at the top of the stairs when Sadie glanced at the red curtain pulled across one end of the attic.

'What's behind there, Em?'

'Don't ask' came the receding voice as Em made her way downstairs.

The heavy velvet drapes looked like they belonged in a theatre.

'Is it a stage?' Sadie asked in mock awe.

'Yes - and Sir John Gielgud has been waiting an awfully long time for his cue'

'No really, what is there?'

Em stopped at the bottom of the attic stairs and thought.

'Stuff from my parent's day, that has been there from day one, as far as I can remember. When my grandmother died, a lot of her stuff was put there I think. Not much, just a few boxes, tea chests? When it was my bedroom I just thought "Out of sight, out of mind" and ignored it. I obviously didn't have your enquiring mind. I'll put something quick and easy from the freezer on for dinner shall I and crack open a bottle of wine? We deserve it'

Yes thanks. Down in a minute' Sadie shouted.

In truth, she was curious about what was behind the curtain. She lifted the old velvet material to one side and hung it on a hook on the wall. It was gloomy in there as the light from the window didn't reach inside. The space went only a few feet back anyway so there wasn't much there like Em had mentioned. Pushed to the right-hand side was an old trunk made of some sort of dark wood with metal strips around it. Sadie bent down to look at the lock. No key in there. She was about to turn away when some impulse made her try the lid. It seemed solid at first but gradually, with a complaining creak, it opened.

It was only half-full, certainly not overflowing with Pirate's Gold as it looked like it should be. There were some books laid at the bottom and she lifted the first few out, reading the titles as she went, they didn't look old and her grandmother's name was written in them. Cookery books, household management, a dictionary. She glanced down and saw that a large Bible-type of book had been revealed and she lifted it out. It was heavy and made of leather-covered wood with metal corners and a metal lock. She tried gently to pull the book open but this obviously did need a key. She scrabbled about in the bottom for a couple of minutes whilst being wary of any resident spiders but there was nothing there.

Maybe Em would know although their conversation five minutes ago made her doubt it. She carried the heavy tome down two sets of stairs and into the kitchen where she was met with a welcome red wine and an enquiring eye from Em.

*

'Well, it looked like Merlin's Book of Spells when you brought it down and I wasn't far wrong was I?'

Sadie and Em were sitting at the cleared table with the open 'Spell Book' before them. It was written in a spidery form of old-fashioned handwriting but could be interpreted quite well, even allowing for the archaic spelling. Sadie's excitement was palpable as she read the inscription on the first page.

'Here be these anciente herbale remedyes, pass'd on from my grandmother and her mother and in turne to the industrie of my mother Agnes Norwood, who helpd and did great and divers things in this village of BRYTHESTONE. This being writ down as intent and to pass on to my only daughter Edyth, in the hope of her keeping this anciente tradition.

Sarah Norwood.'

There were lots of recipes, potions, and remedies as well as many hand-drawn illustrations down the margin. There were drawings of the herbs and flowers they used with their name alongside and even a few drawings of fairies, imps and demons, which admittedly wouldn't have helped in any witchcraft trials held against them! They seemed to be illustrating potions to drive out demons though, rather than conjure them up. Em was particularly taken with one dainty fairy drawing, which she felt was mocking her fat fairy. Nevertheless, she got a pencil and copied down the sketch, for reference.

'These are fantastic' grinned Sadie. 'Look at this, "How to clear sticky eyes '

'You'd probably blind yourself if you tried it today. Besides, we have pharmaceutical eye drops. And doctors' grunted Em.

'Don't be such a grump' There are other things here too. "Cough remedie – ipecacuanha, 2 drachms Paregoric, one syrup of Squills"

'Well, they are plant-based I think but Paregoric is tincture of Opium, so it will certainly make you feel like your cough is better, even if it isn't...'

'You non-believer! I bet these all worked, it said she did great things in the village so she must have been popular. She was probably the local doctor! Look here – "For a fresh complexion... How to make hair shine... How to dream of your future husbande, collect seven herbs by moonlight..."

'There you see, I told you Agnes was a witch'

'Herbal remedies Em, no harm in them. Although I'd certainly check up before using them. And giving young girls a giggle while they picked herbs may not be truthful but it brought a bit of excitement and hope into their lives and didn't do them any harm'

'Unless you count blinding someone by...'

'Em! They wouldn't have written it down and passed it on if it didn't work and Agnes would have probably given it all up and become a nun – or got burned at the stake in those times.'

'Point taken. Well it's yours if you want it. The writer even has your name. Sadie is a corruption of Sarah.'

'I'd love it. I'm thinking I could use this and reinstate a herb garden at...' Sadie remembered just in time that she hadn't told Em about her ideas. Soon, very soon, she would be able to reveal them.

'Well anyway' she finished lamely, 'it may give me a few tips'

'You're going to grow a garden of herbs on the balcony of your London flat?' Em looked incredulous.

'Not quite' smiled Sadie and changed the subject quickly. 'Where would I find the history of this village? The library? Would they have anything that might tell me of the 'Great things' Agnes did for the village?'

'The old library burnt down in the fifties and it's been rehomed in that single-storey red-brick building off the square. Quite a few things were saved though, including the older and rare books. I think the church looked after them, so maybe you could go and have a word with your old mate?'

Sadie realised she was talking about Thomas Poole who had been one of her playmates during those long childhood summers. In fact, he might be the only one still living here and then only because he had returned here to take up the post of vicar of Brytherstone and district. She remembered a very dignified young boy for his age, calm and serious but very kind. He used to amaze the rest of them with his knowledge of the countryside. Whatever birds, animals or insects they saw, Thomas knew all about them. He was an excellent storyteller too and used to sit in Mab's Wood, surrounded by at least six or seven other children and scare them to death with stories of the Spirits of Mab's Wood until they ran back to the lane screaming and laughing.

'I might just do that' she answered 'and when are you telling Meg she can move in?'

'She's coming to dinner tomorrow evening' she smiled because they both knew this meant Meg was cooking it too, 'I thought I'd tell her then.'

'You know' said Em reflectively, 'I feel like I'm pushing you out and I hope you know that's the last thing I want to do'

'I do know that' said Sadie, giving her aunt a hug 'There's room for us all and we all get on well anyway. Besides, I have to go back to London soon but I will be back as soon as I can'

Sooner than you think Em, she smiled to herself.

Chapter 12

The next evening, after a secret trip to Gressleigh, Sadie found herself seated around Em's old kitchen table, waiting for the delicious-smelling food to be dished out. Opposite her was Thomas Poole who was still called Thomas. It had never been Tom or Tommy even when they were children. He was a very precise boy and had grown up to be not much different, which included the warm smile and the kindness and calm that emanated from him. He still wore the metal-rimmed glasses that made him look very wise. After a moment's hesitation, he and Sadie had hugged and the years fell away.

Next to him was his wife Joanna. She had been very mouse-like when she arrived but was now coming round. Sadie could see tell that she was quite shy and wondered how much of a disadvantage this was for a vicar's wife but as she melted, she joined in the conversation and was very knowledgeable about all the varied subjects Em introduced. She was just as lovely as her husband.

Em sat at one end, holding forth on everything under the sun while Meg rushed round, red-faced from the heat but refusing all offers of help. Sadie wouldn't have believed this if she hadn't heard the exchange before the guests arrived when Em asked if she could at least serve the dishes and Meg's voice had risen an octave and she had said 'But it makes me feel *useful* again' – to which Em had no reply.

Eventually, the dinner arrived on the table. Meg didn't do starters, preferring a good hearty meal and something sweet and laden with calories for pudding. The cheesy meatball casserole smelt mouth-watering. Thomas was positively drooling as Meg spooned a generous portion on his plate, which he held forward in an Oliver Twist 'More please' position with an expression to match.

After the meal, including a plum and marzipan tart, had been demolished, mention was made by Em of the history of Brytherstone, in particular the Norwood family. Sadie had guessed as soon as she saw Thomas, why he had been invited but didn't realise the extent of his interest.

'Well Em, as you know, I'm writing a book on Brytherstone history and of course, the Norwood family is inextricably bound up in that history. They were the most important family here for hundreds of years until the Fitzherberts took over their mantle. Norwood was supposed to be derived from North Wood which is the earlier name for Mab's Wood, where we used to play, Sadie. What was that saying Em?'

'There's always been a Norwood in Brytherstone and there always will be' replied Em in a sing-song voice.

'You're the last though Em' Sadie remarked, then coloured up as she realised how tactless she had been. Em had never had children – or indeed married. Although, according to the grapevine i.e. her mother, there had been a few chances. One when she was away at art College and later there was something about the 'big love' in her life that hadn't worked out. Em had never asked about this, as she knew it wouldn't be welcome. Mostly outgoing and gregarious, Em was nevertheless fiercely private when it came to herself. She didn't seem to have noticed Sadie's gaffe though and the conversation continued while Sadie pulled herself together.

'That's the extraordinary thing about the Norwoods' continued Thomas, 'The Norwood name has been carried on through the centuries, passing on to the children, regardless of the paternal name. The very first 'Girl Power' females were the Norwoods. Centuries ago until, well quite recently, the patriarch was all – and the importance of handing down his own name to his progeny was a matter of manly pride.'

Thomas looked around him and smiled his crooked smile, his little piggy eyes lighting up with delight as he regaled his wholly female audience.

'However, in researching the documents regarding the ancestral home, Acorn Cottage, there was a covenant in the deeds that the owner of the house has got to be a Norwood. Not just anyone can change their name to Norwood though; you have got to be a descendant or married to a descendant so your children could carry on the name. This obviously changed things for the males who married a Norwood female and rather than relinquish the farmhouse and its lands – which from the mid-1700s until WWII were extensive- the husbands agreed on this condition. Your grandmother. Em, was a Norwood and your grandfather changed his name.'

'Yes, the awkward caveat. No wonder things are progressing quickly now.' Sadie half-murmured but Em's sharp ears picked it up.

'Awkward caveat? What's going on – and what's progressing?' she asked her niece, leaning forward.

All eyes were now on Sadie. She hadn't quite formulated what she was going to say but it wasn't fair to keep everyone hanging on any longer. She took a deep breath and trusted to fate.

'I've been desperate to tell you all about this' she began, looking directly at Em 'but I had to wait until I had something definite to tell you as I didn't want to get your hopes up. I've been negotiating to buy Acorn Cottage.'

There was a collective intake of breath. Obviously this hadn't even been on their radar, probably because the place had been abandoned so many years it had become part of the landscape. Possibly it was also that she was regarded as a city girl, who wouldn't even want that sort of lifestyle. Sadie wanted to rid them of that thought.

'As soon as I saw it I felt an affinity there. I just felt I belonged somehow. It wasn't even till I asked Em about it that I knew it was anything to do with my family. It was never mentioned by my parents – or by you for that matter Em.'

Em looked stunned.

'For my part, it didn't even occur to me that you would be interested, I suppose just because I wasn't interested myself. That was selfish and now fills me with shame. As for your parents – well, I rather think your mother wanted to disassociate herself from this place and all its connotations.'

'Witches, you mean?' Sadie laughed

'Possibly- but more like the country bumpkin aspect. She was quite happy living in the middle of a city and this part of her life had no meaning any more. She couldn't wait to leave.'

Sadie shook her head.

'No-one is to blame and it isn't a problem. If you had told me about it years ago I might not have appreciated it like I do now. If you had told me even five years ago that I would feel this solid connection with an abandoned old cottage in the back of beyond, I'd have laughed in your face. Yet, connection there was.

'How on earth can you afford it? How did you find the owner?' added an open-mouthed Meg.

Sadie blushed a little.

'I'm afraid I tried a door, which I found open. When I was looking round, there were a few old letters heaped on the side from a long time ago. A few had a company's name on-Besson's- and reading it...' here Sadie had the grace to look embarrassed, 'it was obviously the company who bought the cottage. Nothing personal-just pertaining to the original purchase.

I looked it up on the internet when I got home and amazingly, the same firm is still running but is now run by the original owner's son. They mostly run property services in Spain and Portugal now – and from his surprised tone, Acorn Cottage had fallen under their radar.

I sent him photos of the most dilapidated parts of the house and the overgrown areas of the grounds, as he had never seen it in photos or in person. I took really awful photos but they were actually of part of the property so I don't feel too bad. It looked as though more needed doing than actually does though because it's in pretty good condition considering it's been standing empty. I wasn't going to tell him that though and he didn't even want to send anyone up to see it. To be honest, I think he just wanted it off his hands and any money would have bought it. I made him a low offer, which he hummed and hawed about just to show willing, then accepted it before I changed my mind, which I wouldn't have of course. He asked about land and I said all the land had been sold off well before they purchased it, it was just a large garden. He scrabbled about in the background for a while, and then asked his secretary something and a few minutes later he said, "Good lord, that's a long time ago!" He could see that all the farmland had been sold off and he asked if it just comprised garden and outbuildings to which I said yes, truthfully. They are old cattle sheds covered in poo, I said, just to make it sound even worse. I think he would have paid me to take it off his hands at that stage! He gave me the name of the solicitor who dealt with it all those years ago for my grandfather in Gressleigh, which, although I didn't know it, is our family solicitor still. Em nodded, still dumbstruck, when Sadie said Mr. Huggit asked to be remembered to her.'

Sadie looked at her rapt audience and laughed at the bombshell she had dropped. She went on.

'So, I might as well get it all over with at once. The barns... I had a well-paid job before I worked for Austin and Austin wasn't too mean with the wages I earned from him. I am getting my half of the house I shared with him, which is on the verge of a sale and I am in the process of selling my London flat to Robert, Ali's brother. It is all moving on as we speak. London prices go a long way round here.'

'You said the barns?' Em croaked finding her voice at last.

'Yes, I have plans for artisan workshops there for craftspeople to work in and sell what they make. It's a courtyard and a potential eight units, so maybe you could have a workshop Em, although I'm not sure about the natural light, it may not suit you – but maybe you Meg, a bakery selling your produce? Any sort of crafts from people in the village and district and I would make the rent very reasonable. I've already enquired into planning permission and the first overtures have been looking hopeful.'

'I can't believe you've done all that in the short time you've been here' said Em as everyone beamed at each other. It seemed they thought it was a good idea, fingers crossed.

And *that's* why you've spent all the time on your phone being secretive,' continued Em, 'I was terrified you were getting back with that wazzock Austin!'

'Oh ye of little faith' laughed Sadie, 'What do you think Meg?'

Meg's round apple-cheeked face looked a picture of happiness until she thought of something.

'But I won't be able to bake there will I and I haven't got anywhere else.'

Sadie frowned at Em who clapped her hand to her mouth.

'Meg, I'd forgotten with all this high-class entertainment from Sadie but would you like to move in here with me – for as long as it takes? Until something affordable comes up in Brytherstone?'

Tears sprang to Meg's eyes and Joanna put her arm round her to give her a cuddle.

'Oh Em, if you're sure – and it may take ages for anything to come up here? And what about Sadie?'

'Well, I'm back in London any day now and then back here I'll have my own place won't I?' Sadie smiled 'And I was going to say that if Em's oven can't cope at any point – and let's face it, it hasn't had much practice...'

There was a gasp and a horrified look from Em, spoiled by the laughter in her eyes.

'...that you can use the oven at Acorn Cottage, once it's all been restored, or if that's impossible, replaced. It looks fairly sturdy though. The only payment is in cheese scones.' she grinned.

Meg was beaming from ear to ear and ran across to hug Sadie. When she disentangled herself, Meg hugged Em, then Em hugged Sadie and soon Thomas and Joanna were joining in, with Thomas with tears on his cheeks too.

'I do like a happy ending' he sniffed as everyone laughed.

Sadie realised from their reaction that it wasn't just a madcap scheme, it really could happen and these people were behind her all the way. When she finally escaped from their hugs, Em asked,

'Has any money changed hands? Any signatures on documents?'

'Well yes, it's down in writing that I'm buying Acorn Cottage and outbuildings for the agreed price. I've signed a document at Huggits earlier today to say as much. I sign all the documents when I get back to London – and then it is a waiting game. Although not as long as it could be as Besson's are wanting it off their hands to buy more property abroad and there's no forward chain. My buyer, Ali's brother Robert, is getting the money to me very soon and there is a buyer in the pipeline for mine and Austin's house. Can I ask all of you not to mention it yet? It's been there for years with no one noticing it but I don't want to jinx it by reminding others it's there and have them trying to gazump me!'

'Cross my heart and hope to have a large studio there' announced Em.

Thomas and Joanna promised too- and if you can't trust a vicar and his wife…

Meg agreed enthusiastically but Em caught the fleeting glance on her niece's face. She knew Meg was terrible at keeping secrets just because she forgot they were supposed to be secrets in the first place.

'Don't worry' Em whispered 'If it means her getting her blessed bakery, she'll keep quiet.'

The celebrations, helped by three bottles of sparkling wine hidden by Sadie earlier, went on till after midnight. As they got up to go, Thomas nudged his wife who looked down and said

'No, it's alright Thomas, honestly.'

Thomas looked at Sadie and shrugged his shoulders then seemed to change his mind.

'Joanna is a compulsive knitter. Any spare minute she has is taken up with it; she even designs most of the items herself. I thought it would be a nice idea if she could have one of your workshops?'

'I'm sure there won't be enough to fill a unit.' Joanna said, colouring up.

'None of them are particularly big but just big enough.' smiled Sadie 'You wouldn't need much room to work – mainly just displaying and selling. If you were worried about it though, you could share with someone else in the same position. You could then each pay half the rent.'

'Betty makes lovely felt animals and bags' Joanna gushed, suddenly looking more animated.

'There you are then' smiled Thomas, looking proudly at his wife.

'Just one more thing' said Sadie, looking apprehensively at Em 'This isn't just because of the caveat. I hope you don't mind but I have changed my name legally to Norwood, as I feel that's what it should be.'

Em looked very pleased 'That's how I've always thought of you anyway.' she smiled.

When everyone had gone, Sadie was left feeling very excited because she could actually feel this thing happening. She just knew it would be a success. She grinned at her newfound confidence in life, this optimism that everything she was doing was the right thing to do. Maybe she had inherited second-sight from her 'witchy' ancestors.

Chapter 13

The morning of her departure was glorious and she didn't want to leave. The sun was so warm at 7 am that Sadie had her breakfast outside on the old rickety table. Em was still sleeping and there was no point in waking her as she'd see her later. First though, she wanted to have a last look at her new home before she left. She had, prematurely she knew, arranged for a locksmith to go up tomorrow to make the back door secure for now but she would use the unlocked door one more time to get in today.

Finishing the last of her coffee, she called gently to Whisky, who didn't actually need calling as he was already standing under the hook in the hall where his lead was. Quietly she closed the front door and went out of the village, slightly up the hill, turned right and made her now-familiar way to Acorn Cottage.

Glimpsing the house through the trees lining the driveway, her heart gave an excited lurch. The tall chimneys peeping over the tops now were invisible from the road. Her own private little world. She listened as she walked and all she could hear were her own footsteps, birds singing and strange little snuffling noises from her side which meant that Whisky wanted to be let off the lead. The occasional buzz of an insect passed by her but there was nothing else to disturb the tranquillity of this place. She suddenly felt a pang of regret that she would bring more traffic up the lane at the bottom of the drive with her workshop scheme but realised it could never be too bad. The lane only led to a farm a mile further on so all the activity would be restricted to that small part where the barn was.

She had reached the house and stood for a minute, taking in the mellow, weathered stonework and its wooden porch. Yellow roses were climbing round one of the windows. She loved clichés, she thought with a grin. The porch was falling to pieces and would have to be replaced but apart from that and a good clean, it looked from here like she could move in tomorrow, albeit in a much less comfortable state than she would want.

Turning and looking down the front garden, there were far more flowers out than before. Mauves, pinks, and yellows vied for position in the well-stocked borders. Maybe her prospective new neighbour was keeping an eye on it. Now there was a sobering thought – having Mr Happy as a neighbour. Still, into each life some rain must fall, as Longfellow said. Luckily, the cabin was a field's width away and hopefully they would not meet much.

She went to the back door and was surprised to find it had stuck. She put her foot against the bottom and kicked while pushing the door with her hands. The warm weather must have made the wood swell. She took a deep breath and charged at it with her shoulder. It didn't move and now her shoulder would hurt for the long drive home. She was just rubbing it when an amused voice said, close to her ear,

'It's not stuck, it's locked.'

She swung round to see the smug expression of 'log cabin man'.

'Locked?' she was confused, 'what do you mean locked?'

'I mean a lock has been put on it, with a key that turns, to keep people out.' came the sarcastic reply.

'Has the locksmith been already? He said tomorrow?' Sadie frowned.

She saw the same cloud of confusion pass over his face too and her brain started ticking at last.

'You were going to get a lock for the door' he whispered, half to himself,

'Yes!' she shouted triumphantly, 'because I've bought it. Acorn Cottage is mine. Put that in your pipe and smoke it!'

Sadie's elation at getting the upper hand was cut short by the amused expression in his eyes and the twitch at the corner of his – Oh God – pretty gorgeous mouth. He threw an arm out to indicate the back terrace and followed her round there. Why was she doing as he asked, so meekly? He then indicated the low wall overlooking the grass and the old herb garden and they both sat down. Sadie edged further away as she realised they were too close and he looked amused again – damn him. Disarmingly, he held his hand out to her.

'Raff Maguire, your neighbour I believe. I know you're a Norwood but…'

She thought for a moment then firmly shook his hand.

'Sadie Norwood. My name was actually Barnes, from my father but it is Norwood from now on.'

'Ah, following in the old tradition then?' he smiled.

'You knew about the tradition?'

'Of course, your family history has been inextricably bound up with mine for generations.'

'I didn't know that or indeed anything regarding my family history. I've only just found out about this cottage and my ancestors but I just felt immediately – so close to them.' Sadie finished lamely.

'The Norwoods always did have the sixth sense.' he laughed.

'Don't say you believe they were witches too?' asked Sadie.

'Not witches - witches in the early sense were an invention of over-active and suspicious minds. Herbal healers, yes. Early doctors with their extensive knowledge of what herbs, method and action would help to cure people. The Norwoods were more than that though. They were extraordinary people. Strong, intelligent women -

feisty too- with a way of getting what they wanted.'

He was laughing now and looking straight into her eyes. She knew he was comparing her ancestors with herself and she was coming up favourably, which pleased her more than she would have thought. Annoyingly, she felt herself blushing and to distract him, she found herself garbling.

'Have you got any information on the Norwoods? I would love to hear anything you've got on them. We found an ancient Herbal Remedy book of Sarah Norwood's, centuries-old...'

Stop now Sadie, she thought, before you become a dribbling wreck. She looked up at his kind eyes (why hadn't she noticed that before?) and his lovely sensuous lips turning up at the corners in a very...

'...and Thomas, you know, the vicar? My playmate when I was a child. Glasses, married to...' she burbled on 'is helping me find any records from the church and other old sources. Do you know Thomas?'

Shoot me now, she thought.

'Thomas, of course, one of my old childhood friends. I was very glad when he came back here and he was delighted to be 'posted' here.'

'You were his friend too?' Sadie sounded almost accusatory. What did he mean? He couldn't have been. Yet she was only here on holidays. She wasn't a regular, a local, and perhaps he was? She felt some sadness at the thought. As she looked at Raff, she saw a strange look cross his face.

'Sadie!' he whispered in quiet realisation and shook his head slightly. 'Little red-haired, green-eyed Sadie. I felt I knew you as soon as I saw you but I couldn't work out how. I'm not sure I realised who you were even when we used to play together as children, especially as you had a different name then. Barnes, did you say?'

Then it all came flooding back to Sadie. The tall dark-haired lad, sensible, always at the edge of the gatherings. Essentially a loner but joining in quietly. Looking over the other's heads to meet her eyes. The strange look in his and the thrill it induced in the adolescent Sadie. Her first crush.

'Patrick?' she breathed.

'You remember!' he smiled 'Always called that because it was my father's name but it was really because I hated the name Raphael. I was teased about it mercilessly. I've got used to it now though.'

'Though obviously you prefer Raff?' she countered, smiling back despite herself.

'It's easier.' Raff replied

They held each other's gaze for what seemed like minutes. Remembering how they felt when they were young. Yes, the first stirrings of an adolescent heart.

'I'm very pleased to meet you again Sadie, in spite of our none too promising start.'

'Me too' was all that Sadie could manage but she said it with feeling.

Chapter 14

James stood behind Em, his hands on her shoulders, looking around the inside of Acorn Cottage.

'Doesn't it make you feel anything Em, like it did with Sadie?'

Em stood there for another couple of minutes, then suddenly shut her eyes and took a deep breath in, slowly releasing it while holding her hands in front of her.

'Not a thing!' she winked as James, who thought a mystic transformation was taking place, tutted at her.

'You have no soul' he grinned.

'I freely admit it. It has been said I'm not a typical Norwood and take after my mum more, not in looks, just personality-wise. I don't have the interest in family ancestry that Sadie has or I'd have told her a bit more about it. Although, I believe that wanting to know about your ancestors comes more with age. If I'd tried talking to her about them when she was younger, she'd probably have been too caught up with what was going on in her own life at the time.'

'Very true' said James, 'although in my case, our noble ancestry was hammered into me at an early age and now I'm happy to just forget about it. It's been more of a burden than anything else but I shouldn't moan. In fact I'll stop right now before you give me a lecture.'

'Lecture? Me? I wouldn't presume' said Em innocently while James raised his eyes heavenward, remembering, no doubt, the countless lectures he'd endured from her.

'So, now you have me where you want me' James wiggled his eyebrows 'what is it I can do to help?'

Em looked around the house. Sadie had left the keys with her when she had returned to London for the second time. It was like Sadie thought, a good solid building but in need of a complete refurb to bring it into a habitable condition. She had left a list for Em to give the builders but the real problem was the courtyard.

It needed electric running to it and a couple of toilets and sinks erected in the car park. The car park needed clearing, then repairs and a deep clean on the units were needed too. Sadie had stressed that she wanted the character left in including the cobbles and the stone walls but windows needed putting in all the units and a large double door in Meg's corner unit. Some pointing needed to be done and painting... Em sighed- it would take forever. This is where James came in.

'I'd like to ask a favour. Your workmen at Winterhill Manor...'

'Not technically mine any more but...'

'Don't interrupt! And you know they're all friends of yours anyway. I wondered if they could start early on this. Sadie says she trusts me to hire who I think is best and I think they are best. She has set her heart on getting this all up and running this year and whereas I think it's a mammoth task, I think she's got the energy and drive to see it done.'

'Takes after her aunt then?'

'Oh, you know what I'm like James. I veer between bursts of energy and 'can't be bothered' periods. She's a true Norwood. Sees something she wants and goes for it. I know,' she began, that the workmen are in reserve for the National Trust. They get all their jobs done in winter when the visitors aren't here and only do small maintenance jobs when the house is open. This job would supplement their wages, so you would be helping them out anyway.'

'Yes, I can see the sense in that but, isn't it illegal? This place isn't technically Sadie's yet, she's exchanged but not actually completed, although no one is likely to pull out at this stage. If anyone saw what we were doing, it may spoil things for her. I'm presuming she doesn't know of your scheme.'

'No, because she might have the same reaction as you and I would like to present her with a fait accompli'

'It will take more than a month to do but I suppose we could be well on the way if it would help her.'

'Well, fait half accompli then. It will definitely help and won't seem as daunting when she moves up here to be faced with it all from the start. What do you think? I've got the deep-clean people coming in tomorrow to go through the house.'

James looked at her eager face and did what he always did when faced with this immovable object – he gave in.

'Let me ask them, I'll phone Ernie now and see what he has to say. I'm sure he'll see the others in the pub tonight anyway so he can ask them. He'll know more about the timescale than I do.'

With that he wandered off into the garden and was soon in earnest discussions on his mobile. Em stepped out of the back and felt a small sliver of the feeling that Sadie must have had when seeing this place for the first time. She had been too young to remember much about it but a few things were coming back to her now. Mostly the garden, she couldn't remember going inside that much, she had been told to go and play outside while her parents went and chatted to her grandmother – or put her shopping away. She remembered her mum making a pot of stew and leaving it in the range oven to cook slowly.

She could hear James 'yes-ing and no-ing' to her left and his tone indicated that things were hopeful. Wandering down to what Sadie had laughingly called the Herb Garden and what she, more realistically, called the Mess of Weeds, she gave it an appraisal. She could see how it could be restored and could make out some paths, possibly in the shape of a cross, that would be fairly easy to uncover. The centre was bare and needed something to be a focal point. Her imagination was awakening now after being stuck on the Fat Fairy for so long. At least that had worked out in the end and the Trust loved the Fairy-who-had-been-on-a-diet statue. So did James, which meant more to her than anything else. The more she stared at the Mess in front of her now, the more her brain started to tick over. The beginnings of an idea came to her. She could hear James calling to her now so she mentally reached for the lightbulb above her head and put it away until later.

'They were very keen' beamed James, 'In fact they have no jobs on at Winterhill and have been kicking their heels for the last week. The weather forecast is good so they're raring to go. I've got a decent price for the job, it's all extra for them anyway- and I've promised them sandwiches and flasks of tea and coffee for lunch throughout. I said I'd be on hand, either here or at the other end of a phone, as a sort of project manager. With all the instructions from Sadie (he ruefully held up a big sheaf of printed instructions), we should be able to get on quite well.'

'You're a good man, James Fitzherbert' Em narrowly pulled back from hugging him - it didn't do to be too demonstrative. However, James had different ideas.

'Thank you Madame' he said, pulling her into a bear hug, 'praise indeed from you.'

'Get off you idiot' she pulled away laughing, 'I can be nice when I want. Usually when there's an x in the month.'

'I don't suppose you can be extra nice and say…'

'You're not asking again?'

'Why break the habit of a lifetime?'

'You know the answer' Em was starting to look annoyed so James changed the subject quickly.

'Are you sure about all this' he said, indicating the work list 'because if someone from Besson's does come up here and sees this before the deeds are actually…'

'Don't worry, I'm invoking my ancestor's second sight and they are saying, quite clearly, that all will be well.'

'Well in that case, who are we to argue with them?'

Em strolled back to the village after refusing a lift from James, as she had to give Whisky a walk. He had been spoilt by Sadie's walks and now knew his way up here by himself, not that she would let him of course. She half-wondered if Sadie would want him up here with her, as he loved her company. She looked down thoughtfully at Whisky who returned the look with an offended one of his own. Em suspected it was more as a punishment than anything.

'And when did *you* get second sight?' she asked him grumpily.

As she reached the courtyard, she had another look around but apart from the corner unit, they were all too small for a workshop and had even less light than her own Troglodyte cave back home. Even Meg's corner unit wouldn't have the light coming in where Em needed it. It was a nice idea of Sadie's to have a new studio there but unfortunately, not practical. The thought of workshops brought her back to her Mess of Weeds idea, so the lightbulb came back into being and she walked back home full of plans.

Chapter 15

This was it – the day had finally arrived. It had seemed to be a long time happening but in reality it had been an incredibly smooth operation. She was leaving city life behind her and heading for her new home.

London wasn't the place Sadie remembered it being or maybe she wasn't the person she remembered being when she lived here. Whatever it was, city life had lost any vestiges of glamour that was clinging to it in her mind, to be replaced with the country idyll of her childhood- and that was very soon to become a reality.

Her flat was sold to Ali's brother and the money for it had just been released. Her half-share of Austin's house – she couldn't think of it as hers – from a cash buyer, went into the banks a few days ago. Any time now, after the final completion date today, Acorn Cottage would be hers. She mentally hugged herself at the thought.

These last weeks, in the country's capital city was more than she could stand now. Even when she left the flat and stayed with Ali for the last couple of weeks to give Robert time to decorate it, hadn't made her miss the bright lights. Nor the pollution, the noise and the total busyness of the place.

She had made a journey up to Brytherstone about just after she had returned to London, to hire builders -getting them in place so they could start immediately after she finalised the deal on the place. It was easier said than done, as everyone seemed to be booked up for months ahead. In the end, she had written out a long and exhaustive list of what she needed doing and left it in her aunt's hands. Under normal circumstances, this would have been as sensible as leaving Nero with a violin and a box of matches. Em had promised though, that she would get help in the form of sensible James, whom she was almost sure could help, so Sadie crossed her fingers and toes and left it to Em.

She wanted the courtyard and units done first as they needed to start trading, if possible, while there was still part of the summer season left. The house itself would be just about habitable after a deep clean, although she would stay at Em's until it was decorated and all the jobs were done on her list. She had asked her aunt to get some house-blitzers in as soon as she gave the word, when everything was signed. She had already had the surveyors give it a thorough check and there were, surprisingly, no major issues. Replacing of tiles, replastering where said tile made bedroom wall damp, a couple of the upper windows replacing but nothing that she felt would be overwhelming. It must have been a sturdily built house in the first place and well maintained by her grandfather until he sold it to Besson's.

She had packed her bags, said a fond farewell to Ali and family and had called at the London solicitors to tie everything up. She was now happily facing the long drive north because at the end of it would be Home! She had decided to start again with furniture – nothing she had would suit Acorn Cottage and she was looking forward to going around the second-hand furniture stores to match up the period of the cottage. Which period she didn't know yet but was hoping the furniture she saw would suggest something. All the personal things were crammed into the back and boot of her car though some boxes were left at Ali's with her extensive library of books in that she couldn't part with, as well as some of the bigger things that wouldn't fit in the car. Ali was bringing them up to her soon and she was really looking forward to showing her the cottage. She was sure she'd like it too. She was going to call there on her way back to check it was still okay, like a mother with her baby, and then she could be at Em's in time for tea. She sighed with contentment.

*

The weather had turned by the time she reached Delham, the nearest town to the south of Brytherstone. She dodged the raindrops after pulling into a high-end supermarket car park – Delham was that sort of place- and emerged with three bottles of champagne. Sheer indulgence and extortionately expensive but it wasn't every day you could toast the acquisition of the old ancestral home *and* the beginnings of a new business venture. There was a long way to go before it all came to fruition but she was on the road and going in the right direction, which was literally what she was doing now. A call off at Acorn Cottage to see what needed doing first on Monday, then off to Em's.

As she drew up to the barns and turned into the driveway, she could see a couple of white vans parked there. Pulling into the courtyard, she could hear drilling and hammering. There were sandblasters polishing years of grime from the outer walls and someone was using a pressure cleaner on the cobbles of the courtyard.

Sadie shook her head as if to put her brain back into place. These were all the things on her list that were to be started next week! The biggest surprise though was inside the little units. She crept up to them as though she were a trespasser on her own property because she was so disorientated. The inner stone walls had been cleaned up and disinfected so no one would ever guess that cows had splattered the digested remains of their dinner up them many years ago. They were all clean and new-looking but still retaining their character with newly plastered ceilings. They were looking light inside too although some of the new windows hadn't been fitted yet and were just holes in the wall. She stood inside the third one she looked in, her mouth hanging open in amazement.

'Hiya luv' shouted a friendly voice and she turned to see a man in dark blue overalls covered with tasteful white splodges. He was carrying a bucket and a medieval instrument of torture, which might have something to do with plastering. 'Can I help you?'

'No, it's okay…' then she grinned and held her hand out, 'Sadie Norwood.'

How easy that name came to her now.

'Ah, the boss! Pleased to meet you at last.' he wryly pulled on his cap.

'Can I ask how on earth you've got all this done? I just wasn't expecting…'

'You'd better be talking to Sir James about that I reckon. I think he'd want to tell you himself. Besides if you're going to tell anyone off, I'm not putting myself forward!' he gave an exaggerated wink before he started whistling and examining the ceiling.

'No, it's all – wonderful!' she laughed. She shook her head again to dispel any thoughts that she might have somehow turned into the wrong driveway, then got back into the car and carried on up to the cottage.

James was there, looking a bit sheepish. He held his hands up as if to ward off blows.

'How…?' she began and then just threw her arm out towards the courtyard in dumb disbelief.

James crinkly blue eyes narrowed in amusement and he chuckled.

'Your aunt, of course,' he began as Sadie nodded in acquiescence, 'we hoped you wouldn't mind and she thought it would be a nice surprise when you got back, You know what she's like'

Sadie, astounded as she was, couldn't help noticing the pride with which he said the last few words.

'I do indeed,' she laughed 'and it really is the most brilliant surprise. It's a good job it didn't all fall through though or we'd have been doing it up for the next owner's benefit.'

'Oh we were 99.9% certain. Your solicitor in Gressleigh is a personal friend of mine - old school chum- and I asked him to keep us up to date. We probably knew more than you did about how the sale was coming along.'

He laughed out loud at the expression of shock, disbelief and sheer happiness on Sadie's face.

'You'll soon get used to Yorkshire country ways. We usually do what we want if we think we can get away with it. Going to Em's now?'

'Yes I am but I actually feel like I'm in a state of shock. Is hot sweet tea still good for that? You've given me a marvellous head start, I just can't thank you all enough. There's only the house to get started on now.'

She watched James' expression as if in slow motion. Surely not?

'The house cleaners really got stuck in' he started almost apologetically, 'Made a big difference. You wouldn't believe how much lighter it is inside after three inches of dirt was removed from the windows. Would you like to see…?'

'No, no, I'll er, come up tomorrow. There's just too much to take in and I need a sit-down and a glass of wine before it all morphs into reality in my head. You have been so good, I can't thank you enough. You have obviously overseen it and I'd like to pay you accordingly if you won't be offended?'

'Don't you dare!' he said in mock anger. 'I've loved it. It's given me a sense of purpose which has been missing for a long while. I'll be sorry to see it finished, not for your sake, of course.'

Sadie reached out to hug him and he came away pink-faced and pleased. As she turned back to her car, something caught her eye at the front door.

'Oh!' she gasped.

'Ah yes, the new porch. Raff said the old one was rotten and dangerous. You could put your finger through some of the wood. So he's made a new, more substantial one out of oak. You know,' he added 'to go with Acorn Cottage.'

'It's beautiful.' she sighed, admiring the beautifully carved uprights, not squared off but with natural curves to them as though he had followed the lines of the oak itself rather than making it uniform.

'You think *that's* beautiful, you wait till you see… Ah, it's a secret.' James looked suitably embarrassed, 'I'm not awfully good at secrets.'

Sadie grinned and resisted the urge to hug him again. He looked so crestfallen.

'All will be revealed later, I expect.' she smiled.

Driving towards Em's, she could feel this place embracing her. Village hugs or not, her eyes were feeling heavy and despite all the excitement, all she wanted to do was sleep but first, she wanted food, wine and a good natter with her aunt- and Meg of course. She found herself hoping for Meg's cooking rather than Em's – and she knew Em would be in complete agreement. She felt blessed and ridiculously happy. She was weeks ahead of where she thought she would be with Acorn Cottage, she had good friends here as well as the one person who epitomised family for her and she was back in Brytherstone, this time for good.   Even the person she had thought might have been a fly in the ointment of her happiness -Raff- seemed to have undergone a personality transplant. Things were definitely looking up. She was back in her spiritual home.

Chapter 16

The sunlight hit her directly between the eyes. Her eyes were only half-open as she tentatively explored where she was. Flat? Ali's? Em's? A voice thundered up two flights of stairs, leaving her in no doubt as to where she was.

'You up yet? Meg's got homemade bread and strawberry jam waiting – and there's a certain dog who's been turning in circles outside your bedroom door for the last twenty minutes.'

Sadie lifted her head off the pillow an inch or two and indeed, she could hear scuffling noises from the landing accompanied by a disgruntled whine. Going downstairs as she was, which in this case meant in a Winnie-the-Pooh nightie, she padded into the kitchen, narrowly avoiding the furball himself who had already tried to trip her up down the stairs and was now threading his way in and out of her legs.

'Don't you ever take him for walks?' she grunted at Em.

'Of course. When I remember but he seems to prefer you for some reason.'

'Probably because I actually take him for a walk and don't just nip down the road to the newsagents.' laughed Sadie.

Em faked a hurt look. 'Can I help it if he has an addiction to Kennel Club Weekly?'

'Sit down you two' grinned Meg, 'you're both as bad as each other.'

'Haven't you had breakfast either Em?'

'No, I've been in the workshop though.'

'Ah, how is the Fat Fairy coming on?'

'Finished her. Put her on a strict diet and just got on with it after James talked some sense into me. It's up at Winterhill Manor in situ; I'll take you up there sometime if you want to see it?

Was it Sadie's imagination or was there a faint blush on Em's cheeks when she mentioned James? She glanced across at Meg who smiled but almost imperceptibly shook her head. Point taken. James though eh? She hoped so, they went so well together in a chalk-and-cheese sort of way.

'Your key is hanging up in the hall' Em continued, 'I hope you don't mind but we had another two cut what with the builders, the cleaners, Raff…'

'I'm glad you did, it makes things easier.' Sadie paused. 'Mr. Miserable seems to be undergoing a personality transplant.'

'Raff? Do you mean Raff? He can be grumpy at times I know and his quick temper probably comes from his gypsy heritage but he's genuinely pleased that the house and barns are being restored, especially by a Norwood. He'll be your new neighbour, did you know?'

'Not that near, thank goodness'

'Whatever has the poor lad done to you?'

'Shouted at me for being on the property and changed my locks before I had a chance and' she cast about for something else 'he set his dog on Whisky.'

'Bran? You couldn't set him on anyone without him licking it to death first. I wondered why they seemed so friendly when they met at the newsagents just recently.'

'When Whisky was picking up his copy of Kennel Club Weekly?' smiled Sadie, innocently.

'You know, Raff was only looking out for Norwood property. *Your* property. He was doing you a favour when you think of it.' said Em.

Sadie didn't want to think about it or about those dark Gypsy looks he'd obviously inherited. She'd thought he looked Italian but those blue eyes were wrong.

'He owns the Gypsy caravan in the clearing. Been in his family for many years.'

Sadie sipped her coffee thoughtfully. So wasn't that her land then – or her caravan? This might cause complications she could do without.

'Does he own the clearing too then?' Sadie wondered if that was perhaps no-man's land between their properties.

'I think it was used as a shared right of way, I'm really not sure. Isn't it on your deeds? You'll have to ask Raff about it, you know I don't listen to important things.'

Sadie hoped it wasn't going to be a bone of contention between them. She stopped herself from going down that route by buttering her last slice of bread. Before she could pick it up, Em had pinched it.

'Hey, I was looking forward to that.' she shouted after her aunt's back as she disappeared into the workshop.

134

'Plenty more here love' said Meg, dropping another slice, thickly buttered, onto the empty plate.

'How are you doing Meg?' asked Sadie. Meg was so kind and uncomplaining that it was easy to forget she was virtually homeless.

'I'm fine. It's lovely living here – and your old room is so cosy. I feel very guilty…'

'Don't you ever think that' she admonished. 'Em loves having you here and I'll soon be living in my cottage.'

'If you need any help, I'd be more than willing. I've always been busy up to now; I'm at a bit of a loose end with no baking.

'You'll be busy again as soon as the units are finished and fitted out and it won't be too long now by the looks of it. I would always accept offers of help but this morning, I'm just going up there for a recce.'

Finishing the last mouthful, she dashed up to shower and dress then went out onto the street with a very impatient Whisky.

*

She called off at the Courtyard first. Even though it was Saturday, some of the workmen were still working. Another unit had been plastered out and when she stood in the middle of

135

the courtyard, she could see that the roof looked like new.

'We used most of the original tiles' came a voice from behind her and a tall, thin man of about sixty walked up to her.' All they needed was a good clean, get rid of the moss and such. We replaced the broken ones with new of course but you can't really tell the difference can you?'

You couldn't at first glance, not unless her visitors stared at them critically but she was hoping they would have more things to look at than the roof tiles.

'It looks fabulous, it was sagging in places so I didn't know if you'd have to end up replacing it all.'

'That was the timbers and we have had to replace a lot of those but the lads have made a good job of it.' He was rightly very proud of their work.

'Thank you so much for getting all this done - and in super-quick time too. I'm so grateful!'

The man smiled and looked relieved at her words. Nodding, he went quietly back to his work.

It *was* all coming together, faster and better than she ever imagined. However, she hadn't seen the inside of the house yet. This was the most important thing though, getting the courtyard up and running. As long as she could move in before Christmas, she would be happy. If Em could put up with her that long. Em didn't say anything but she had lived by herself for so long that Sadie didn't know if she was happy or not about the sudden influx of residents at Church View.

As she reached the top of the driveway, Whisky's ears pricked up and he gave a loud yelp, which made Sadie's eardrums vibrate painfully. Suddenly there was an answering bark, much deeper. Bran! As he was straining at the leash, she gave him his freedom and he shot off like a ferret up a drainpipe.

Sadie wandered up to the front door, fishing in her pocket and wondering which of the keys was for which door, when she came to an abrupt halt. What had been Raff's gorgeous oak porch yesterday had been transformed into a thing of beauty. The gable end of the porch, the inverted 'V', which had been open before, now had a wonderful carved frieze attached to it. She couldn't drag her eyes from it. In the centre was an oak tree, its branches hanging over and sheltering the grass below it. All around in a border, carved acorns grew on branches twining sinuously along the edges. At the base of the oak tree, standing proud of the wood, were the words 'Acorn Cottage'.

She was still taking it all in a couple of minutes later when she was vaguely aware of someone at her side. She turned slowly and met with a pair of amused blue eyes.

'My gift to you – and Acorn Cottage- for bringing it back to life.' he said as Sadie just continued to stare at him until he looked a little worried. 'Do you like it?'

In answer, her bottom lip wobbled and, very embarrassingly, she burst into tears. Raff didn't seem to know what to do but settled for putting a hand on her shoulder and squeezing.

'Well,' he smiled 'if it upsets you that much…'

She tried to speak but a strangled sob came out.

'…I can always take it down and find another Acorn Cottage sign?'

Damn him, he was finding this amusing. Sadie finally pulled herself together.

'I am just so incredibly moved by it. Not just the fact that it is an amazingly beautiful carving in itself but that it represents Acorn Cottage so perfectly. Seeing it has made me realise that this place is mine and I feel that my ancestors would be as delighted as I am.' she sniffed. 'And you must let me pay you.'

'I wouldn't hear of it. I have really enjoyed carving it – and your reaction gives me far more satisfaction than any payment could.'

Raff's hand was still on her shoulder and they realised it at the same time, both stepping backwards like they'd been burnt.

'I love your work, I didn't realise this is what you did.' she garbled. It was more for something to say than anything but it was also the truth. '- and to think, at one point I was going to ask you if you'd stay on to look after the garden'.

Raff smiled, 'Well, I suppose I did give you that impression, carrying pruners round on my shoulder. That was on a strictly amateur basis, I just didn't want to let the old place go to rack and ruin.'

'For which I am eternally grateful.' she said wholeheartedly.

'Perhaps you'd like to see some more of my work? I have a few more commissions in progress in the barn.'

'Oh I'd love that, just let me know when.'

'How about tomorrow? Meet me at 11 a.m. at the Vardo - The Gypsy caravan?'

Sadie wasn't expecting a definite invitation. She thought he was just being polite but she couldn't stop herself from feeling stupidly pleased.

'That would be great.' she said and as he nodded and turned to collect Bran, she added 'and a huge thank-you again.'

When he turned round to her and gave her a genuinely happy smile, her treacherous heart did a backwards somersault.

Chapter 17

Somewhere on the periphery of her mind, Em registered a noise. She ignored it. A moment later it was there again and this time she glanced up to see James walking hesitantly into her workshop from the outer door.

'Grmmf' she said through clenched teeth and hoped that it came out as an expression of annoyance.

'I'm sorry' offered James who could obviously translate Em-speak, 'I did knock.'

Em got on with her sculpture.

'Erm, I know you don't like interruptions to your work' he halted briefly but she didn't deny it, 'but I wondered if I might have a word?'

'Not now James, I'm busy.' she snapped. Why did she do this? She really didn't mean to but he seemed to invite it sometimes. It was easy to be mean to James and she hated herself for being like this to – and there was no other way of describing it – the nicest man she had ever known. She knew why she was like this of course but she continued to kid herself.

'Yes, I see. Well, I'll just go and...' he said quietly and she looked up again as he was opening the door to go out. Her heart, her seemingly cold heart, melted at the sight.

'Oh James, I'm sorry. Please come back. I just wanted to get this right for Sadie. Come over here and tell me what you think. Not finished yet of course.' she held her hand towards him in a conciliatory gesture and James, being James, beamed and came towards her with no recriminations on his tongue or on his mind.

Standing back, she watched his face as he cocked his head from side to side like a giant blond puppy and then walked around it.

'Well come on then, the suspense is killing me!' she shouted.

James looked up at her and smiled. 'I like to take my time.'

He grinned boyishly and to her intense embarrassment, she blushed. He had a certain way of looking at her, which made her turn to jelly. Damn the man.

'I love it, it's perfect. You have the knack of instinctively bringing stone alive. This will be perfect for the cottage.'

Em felt pleased although she tried very hard not to.

'But what's this in the middle?' he went on 'This stone you're working on now?'

'That is a surprise, even from you. And don't forget the whole thing is meant to be a surprise. I know you.' She caught a glimpse of something fleeting passing over James' face. 'You haven't already said something have you? For heaven's sake, she hasn't even been back twenty-four hours!'

James shuffled his feet and looked down at them as though they had suddenly become extremely interesting.

'I might have mentioned, briefly and not very loudly, something about a surprise,' he heard Em start to say something very rude 'but she was looking around her so I don't think she heard – and she has no idea what – or who and if she didn't mention it last night then…'

'It sounds like you've just about got away with it. James, you really are the limit.'

He looked so crestfallen that she put down the chisel, brushed the white dust off her hands and smiled at him.

'Come on, let's go into the kitchen and I'll make us a coffee. You can tell me what you wanted a word about.'

'Lead on.' he laughed as he followed her and then came to a surprised halt as he came into the kitchen. 'Oh, I haven't been in here for a while. It looks, well it looks…'

'Clean? Tidy? Ordered? Welcoming?' offered Em as he struggled for a word. 'Have you forgotten Meg is living here now?'

'Ah, that's why.' said James innocently.

'What are you trying to tell me James? Is there something you'd like to get off your chest about my housekeeping skills?'

He laughed. 'It was always welcoming, even if you couldn't find anything you wanted. It always felt nice.'

Mollified, Em put the kettle on and when they were sitting at a clear and scrubbed kitchen table with their coffees, Em went on.

'She put up with it for a few weeks, Meg I mean, because she said it was my home and she didn't want to interfere but she must have snapped. I came home from a memorial-transporting trip to York and she'd blitzed the place. I thought I'd walked into the wrong house.' she explained to James who chuckled quietly.

. 'I was mad at first – how would I ever find anything again? I knew which pile things were under and how far down the pile they were. Meg stopped me mid-moan and said if I wanted her to cook, which she was more than happy to do, then she had to be able to find things in the place they should be and it was either that or no food, so make my mind up, quickly!. Apparently what tipped her over was finding a small casserole dish in the workshop, full of masonry sealer with the egg whisk sitting in it. She accused me of taking all the kitchen apparatus at some time into the workshop for various evil uses.'

'And was that true?'

'Of course it was but that's not the point.'

'Of course it is.'

'Oh alright then, if you're both going to gang up on me. Mea culpa. I admitted I was wrong and apologised. To my surprise, I quite like living in some sort of order. I just never seem to have time to make it so myself.'

'Where is Meg now?' asked James.

Em sighed. 'She caught the bus into Gressleigh to look for accommodation again. I wish she'd realise that this is her home for as long as she wants. I keep telling her.'

'Pride, Em. Something you should understand more than anyone. She doesn't want to impose on you even though we know she isn't. Can you imagine what you'd be like in the same position?'

'Point taken.' replied Em.

James drained his cup and stood up to go.

'I'm on my way to check Acorn Cottage and see how the work is coming along for Sadie.'

'You're such a good man James.' then she quickly busied herself with clearing the cups away as she saw the look of happy surprise on his face. Then she remembered. 'Hang on; what were you going to tell me?'

'Ah yes, the reason I actually came here in the first place' he smiled, 'You know you mentioned having a party or a dinner for Sadie to celebrate her moving up here? To say welcome to Brytherstone? I wondered if you wanted to hold it at Winterhill Manor?'

'Oh, would you be able to? Doesn't it belong to the National Trust now?'

'Yes, but it's used for weddings, functions, business meetings etc. No reason why this can't be one of those, if unofficially. And we'll be holding it after the place has closed for the evening obviously – so who's to know?'

'You little devil James, I didn't know you were a rebel.' she teased.

'Next Saturday be alright? Gives us time to get people together and get her settled in. I know she will have been here a week but that's not the point is it?'

'Of course it is.' shot back Em.

'Touché' laughed James 'and do you think you can manage to keep it a secret from her?

He ducked out of the door before the dishcloth hit him.

Chapter 18

It was just before 11 am when Sadie reached the caravan. She hadn't wanted to appear too eager so she'd just strolled up from the cottage where she'd arrived over half an hour ago. She'd used the time to look around the rooms. She didn't feel like she'd taken it all in yesterday as her mind was full of carved oak trees and acorns but she had noticed the amount of light now flooding into the place. She had always thought of old cottages as being dark and dingy but all this had needed was the windows cleaning. It would still be light on a dull winter's day – or so she hoped.

The rooms smelt of lemons, the cleaning products she supposed and everything in the rooms and especially the kitchen had been scrubbed to within an inch of its life. There were flagstones in the kitchen but all the wooden floors had been sanded after the cleaners came in and were now ready to be treated. There was a thin layer of dust from the floors but she would hire the cleaners again before she moved in anyway, after the decorating. The paintwork was clean and ready to be painted and the sparkling windows were bare and just ready for newly sanded and painted shutters in the front-facing rooms to make them perfect. The window seats in these rooms looked so inviting; she couldn't wait to have the padded seats made for them.

She had called in this morning a) because she could – because it was hers. Hurrah! And b) because she wanted to think of colour schemes for soft furnishings. Next week she would have to go round the shops in Gressleigh and Denham, sourcing new/old furniture and she was really looking forward to it.

Now, outside the Gypsy caravan, she looked at her watch but then heard an excited bark. She looked down and realise Whisky wasn't there and then saw the two canine friends scampering about in front of Raff who was walking slowly towards her. Her heart did that funny 'ba-bam' thing, which she really wished it wouldn't.

'Am I late?' he said pointedly looking at the watch on her wrist.

'No, I was a bit early, just called in the cottage for a look around' she replied, one word running into the next.

'What do you think?' he said, nodding towards Acorn Cottage.

'I think it's wonderful. Everyone's made a great job on it – and the courtyard. Have you seen the courtyard?'

'Yes, they've really cracked on. That's down to James; he seems to get the most out of people by the 'being unreservedly kind' method. The workmen don't want to let him down because he's so…'

'Nice?' Sadie smiled.

'I know they say it's an overused word but it really does describe him well.' he shrugged with a grin.

'He's a treasure' agreed Sadie.

'That too' said Raff, 'I just wish those two would stop pussy-footing around.'

'Which two?' said Sadie, puzzled.

Raff turned and looked at her askance. 'James and Em. Don't tell me you haven't noticed? I thought women were supposed to have intuition over that sort of thing.'

'Well, I know they're good friends,' she said huffily 'and I did catch there was something between them. Remember I'm not here all the time – or haven't been up to now – to see them. I was thinking yesterday that they would be good together. They sound like an old married couple sometimes anyway. How long, do you think?'

'Have they known each other? Forever I think, since they were children. They apparently went to the same school until James was sent away to boarding school later on.'

'I meant how long have they been together?'

'I don't think they are, that was my point. Everyone thinks they are because they look so 'together', it's so obvious when you see them. To most people anyway.' his lips twitched as he looked down at her.

Stung by the remark, Sadie hurriedly moved the conversation on.

'So, the caravan. Em says it's yours. Are you going to restore it?'

'That's my plan. Do you want to see inside?'

He produced a strange-looking T-shaped key and pushed open the door. Well if the steps would take his weight, they would take hers.

'Oh,' Sadie exclaimed, 'it's not derelict! It's clean and, well, liveable. I expected cobwebs, rot and chaos!'

She looked at the interior. A high bed at one end with a window just above the mattress, a painted chest of drawers – a bookcase with a few books, a bench seat that may have had storage underneath and some sort of a stove with a chimney going up through the painted roof. The paintwork was all ornate but slightly faded.

Raff smiled enigmatically. 'No, I like to keep it clean and in good condition inside. I sometimes use it when I need to feel close to my ancestry. It's the outside that needs restoring the most as it's subject to the weather. Although it's sheltered in this glade, wind, rain and time have still dimmed its former glory. I'm looking forward to doing it; I do a little when I can.'

Raff looked miles away, lost in his thoughts. Sadie's next words brought him back to earth.

'So, it's your caravan but whose land is it?'

His head whipped round.

'Yours' he spat defensively, 'Is there a problem?'

Sadie took an involuntary step backwards.

'No, no, not at all. I was just clarifying that's all. It's all new to me.' she gulped.

Raff's shoulders relaxed visibly and he had the grace to look embarrassed.

'Look, why don't you come back to my place, I'll get you some lunch and I can tell you the story of the Norwoods and the Maguires? '

Sadie pretended to think for a few seconds.

'Yes thank you, I'd like that' and she followed him along the edge of the field towards his cabin, both of them preceded by two happy dogs.

*

Sadie had been treated to a viewing of some of the wonderful woodcarvings and commissions in the big barn -he really was a talented artist - and was now seated on the upstairs balcony of Raff's cabin. She wasn't a fast worker as it wasn't a bedroom. It was an upside-down house to take advantage of the views over the trees. The balcony led from the kitchen and had a small table and two chairs on it, one of which was occupied by Sadie. She could look over the whole of Mab's Wood down to the valley below it. If she turned around, she could see Brytherstone nestling to her left.

She had been seated opposite Raff, sipping coffee and trying to avoid looking into those mesmerising eyes. He was now in the kitchen making their lunch. Sadie looked out over the trees and felt more at peace than she had for a long time. Everything seemed to be falling into place.

'Earth to Sadie' came a deep voice in her ear, which made her go all shivery. 'I asked if you liked dressing on your salad?'

'Sorry, erm, not bothered really.'

He'd told her everything was home-grown so it probably didn't need it anyway. He put a dish down on the table and went back for some delicious-looking bread, which appeared to be homemade. He'd make someone a lovely husband; she thought and grinned to herself. Raff glanced at her and shook his head.

'This all looks yummy' she said and meant it. There were new potatoes, sweet tomatoes, cucumber and crunchy lettuce. There was a side dish of sliced peppers: a chunk of crumbly cheese on a board with a slab of butter and some boiled eggs in a bowl, probably from the chickens she'd noticed on the way in. Afterwards, she leant back against her chair.

'Full up' she said as he offered her another glass of wine.

'It's wine' he said, 'it's not filling.'

'Do you make that as well?' she asked, half-joking but she wasn't really surprised when he said yes. 'Go on then, just one more – it *is* tasty.'

He offered her a bowl of apples.

'From your own tree?' she couldn't help asking.

'No, from yours actually. I pinched a few of the early ones as it's a shame for them to go to waste.' he grinned.

'Oh well, in that case' then she pulled back 'They're not sour are they?'

He took one of the apples and bit into it, then held it out to her to take a bite. At the same time as she was thinking 'Whoa, intimate', she leant forward and bit into it, the sweet juices running down her chin.

'Mmm' she managed ecstatically. Raff looked amused.

'You know' he said 'this is how Adam and Eve started.' and wiggled an eyebrow suggestively.

Was he flirting? Oh my god! Sadie's vocabulary seemed to have deserted her so to fill the silence; she took a huge gulp of the wine to wash the apple down. Then she started coughing. Then choking. Raff, who had at first been laughing, suddenly looked serious.

'Are you alright?'

She wanted to say 'Of course I'm not you complete idiot, I'm choking to death.' But instead took a long intake of breath which didn't help in the slightest.

'Jesus!' shouted Raff and pulled her up, slapping her back but as she was turning a funny colour, he grasped her from behind and did the Heimlich manoeuvre on her. She felt the piece of apple dislodge and could at last breathe out but unfortunately it came out as a coughing fit, which turned her bright red and sent tears streaming down her cheeks.

Suddenly, she felt two strong arms lift her up and hang her over the breakfast bar, then she felt herself being pulled back and for a confusing minute wondered why she was so dizzy until she realised she was hanging upside-down with Raff holding her up by her ankles while saying 'Breathe, breathe, breathe!'

'What are you doing?' she managed to croak.

There was a lull in the 'Breathe' mantra and she could feel Raff go very still.

'You're okay then?'

'I will be when I'm the right way up.' she rasped.

He gently let her down onto the floor, where she collapsed in an untidy heap, feeling very silly and annoyed with herself.

'You couldn't kill me by apple so you're trying the upside-down torture method?' she asked.

'I'm actually trying to save your stupid, ungrateful life.' Raff looked furious and more than a little embarrassed.

Sadie frowned back at him. She'd made a complete fool of herself nearly choking on his apple – well technically, her apple – he'd laughed at her, hit her, squashed her and then held her upside-down like a bungee jumper. So why did she feel like laughing? A snort escaped from her, and then a short bark of a laugh and then a full-on giggle until she couldn't stop.

It looked like Raff thought she was having another choking fit at first but then his mouth twitched at one side, then a huge grin spread over his face, then he was laughing too, his head thrown back. After they had wound down, Sadie held her throat.

'Ow' she said 'It's so sore both with choking and laughing'

He went to fetch a glass of water for her. It felt so good; slipping down a gullet that felt like it had spiky gravel in it.

'You're sure you're okay?' he asked solicitously.

'Fine- but if it's okay with you I'd better get back because I'm only going to be able to croak to you instead of talk. Besides, I didn't tell Em I wouldn't be back for lunch.'

'Not that she'd notice.' Raff smiled.

'True but Meg would. I should have phoned. Please, I'd love to know the story of our families and we hadn't got round to it. Can we...?'

'Yes, we'll make it next time. Now stop talking.' he ordered.

She nodded. Next time, that sounded nice, although she'd made such an idiot of herself, would she dare face him again when she'd had time to think about it?

He was just letting her out of the lower door to collect Whisky from the garden when she realised that, as it was a hot day (and let's face it, she was trying to impress him,) she had put on a light, floral, cotton tea-dress instead of her usual jeans. She looked slowly up at Raff.

'Tell me you didn't see my knickers when I was upside down?' she said, horrified.

Raff tutted. 'Sadie, I was trying to stop you from turning a deeper shade of blue and from dying in my kitchen. Why would I look at your knickers, for heaven's sake?'

'Sorry, sorry' she apologised, 'it's just that I don't normally wear dresses and I suddenly realised that...well, anyway. Thank you for lunch. And for saving my life, which you actually did.'

'Pleasure for both. Anytime.' he smiled.

She collected a reluctant Whisky from his playmate's side and walked over to the field path.

'Sadie.' shouted Raff. 'Very virginal though'

'What?' she frowned 'What is?'

'Your white silky knickers.' he grinned and turned back to the cabin.

Sadie squeezed her eyes together then turned and marched down the path. Damn him, now she really wouldn't dare face him again. Then she stopped and screwed her eyes up again, trying to remember what she'd put on this morning. Then she lifted her dress up to check, in case he was joking and dropped it again. White and silky. She sighed and carried on down the path.

Chapter 19

Much as Em wanted to go to Acorn Cottage with Sadie, she had a commission to finish off and Sadie's gift to get on with. She also had a lot of arranging to do for Saturday's dinner and had been hoping to phone round while Sadie was out. There was no getting away with it though. Sadie thought Em was 'burying yourself in that damp, dingy workshop' and needed to get out for some fresh air. Em hesitated to remind her she'd been burying herself in that workshop almost every day for thirty years. Having said that, she was right about the fresh air and she knew she should be supporting her niece in her new venture and new home.

They were at this moment looking round the sitting room, where Sadie was telling her she was going to paint the wall over the lovely stone fireplace in a midnight blue. She was also going to paint the other walls in a 'sort of creamy ivory' to contrast, apparently. The window seat would be a dark blue print with contrasting cushions. How interested Em was in home furnishings was reflected in the state of her own décor – but she managed to make the right noises in all the right places. She could see the excitement in the younger woman's face and if interior design was what it took to make her happy, then so be it.

Em was so glad to see the old Sadie back again – and very glad to see the old Sadie back in Brytherstone again too. She had always been close to her niece. She'd have made a lousy mother, she was too self-centred and would freely admit it but she didn't think she'd made a bad job of being an aunt.

They had been upstairs where she had seen the reconditioned cast-iron bath, which had been put in originally just after the First World War. Sadie had discussed having all-white walls and soft furnishings in her bedroom for a Swedish look – 'because there's nothing wrong with virginal white' Sadie had huffed to Em's puzzlement.

Now they were walking through to the kitchen where Sadie launched into how the very pale sage green paint would 'lift' the room and make it even lighter. Em could see that now the old net curtains had been done away with from the windows and French doors, that the light flooded in here anyway. She had to admit, for someone who wasn't known for their finer feelings, that she recognised this house had a lovely ambience to it. She also wasn't one for the whole ancestral thing like Sadie was but she did feel a little closer to her ancient family now than she had ever done before, mainly because she hadn't given them a thought until now.

There I go, thought Em; I'll be talking to them soon. I'll be as crazy as old Mrs Bentham with her séances. Is there anybody theeeere? She suddenly became aware that Sadie had asked her something.

'Sorry, what did you say?'

'I should have noticed that your eyes had glazed over long ago,' laughed Sadie fondly.

'No honestly, I'm really interested.' said Em, bending the truth, 'I was just thinking about the ancestors.'

Sadie looked sceptical.

'And the green you were mentioning – lovely.' Em floundered.

'Em, I remember having a conversation with you about paint colours and you said "Why don't they say dark yellow instead of saffron sunset – or light blue instead of Mediterranean sky?"'

'True,' remembered Em 'but your very light whatever-it-was green will look lovely in here. I can't believe the difference in the amount of light in here.

'Speaking of which', smiled Sadie, 'follow me.'

Em dutifully followed her out of the side door and down a small slope at the side and they came to a halt outside the old dovecote. Em was surprised again at the size of it, she couldn't remember it being this big when she was a child, although they had been warned not to go near it. They walked around to the side facing away from the house where there was a direct view over a field to Mab's Wood. Sadie pushed open the huge door.

It was more the size of a small windmill than a dovecote. Indeed, it may have been used for the former purpose originally as there were no nesting holes. It was just the round shape of it, which earned it the nickname of the Dovecote. The interior had been dry enough to use for storage.

'No dove poo then? 'she came out with, which sent Sadie into a fit of giggles.

'Is that all you can say? No dove poo?' she laughed.

'First thing that came to mind.' said Em honestly 'Look up there, I think part of the roof collapsed at some point – we were always told not to play near it – and they've replaced it with a solid wood one. They used to store gardening tools and stuff in here at one time I think. What are you going to do with it? '

For an artist, Em had little imagination when it came to architecture so she was stuck when Sadie asked her what *she* would do with it.

'Me? No idea. Roof's about fourteen or fifteen feet above us I imagine. Maybe had another floor at one time? Might need patching up but then I suppose you could use it for storage too. Garden tools? Maybe a woodshed?

Sadie tutted at her. 'Well, what would you think if I rough-plastered the walls, painted them white to let the light bounce off them – and let lots of light in by making that door a double glass door which can be opened on sunny days?'

'Lots of trouble for a storage space but yes, it would let more light in.' said Em, looking around her.

'So,' Sadie asked 'If I was to not bother replacing the wooden roof and just get rid of it …?'

'You'd have very wet garden tools'

'… and replace it with a glass roof, toughened glass, enabling the light to come flooding down to the floor space?'

Em stood still. Yes, with that and the glass door it would make a big difference to this place. A big difference, she thought and began to turn slowly around, taking it all in.

'But why would you go to all that trouble and expense for a storage space?' she asked.

'Em!' Sadie was half-exasperated and half-amused, 'it's not going to be a storage space. I thought – I hoped – that it could be your new studio.'

Em stared at her open-mouthed and then looked around her again, this time with different eyes. This place was twice as big as her workshop at home and it would be over twice as light as that murky old hole too. She wanted to burst out crying which was most unlike her. She wondered if she might be coming down with something. She saw Sadie's eager, expectant face and reaching out her arms, drew her in for a huge hug.

'I think, Sadie Norwood, that is the best idea you've had since you decided to move up here.' she sniffed and stepped back, 'but you can't go to all that expense just for me.'

'Stop right there! This is my only way to pay you back for all you've done for me over the years and – because you're my brilliant, favourite ever aunt.'

They hugged each other tightly for a while, both sniffing this time and then they disentangled.

'I'm your *only* aunt' whispered Em, swallowing hard.

'You'd still be my favourite aunt, even if you weren't the only one' laughed Sadie through her happy tears.

Chapter 20

The taxi was outside with Em and Meg already waiting in it. Sadie couldn't understand the rush. The dinner Em had booked was for 8pm and it was only 6.50pm now, with the restaurant in Gressleigh under 20 minutes' drive away. However, she was ready now thanks to Em's chivvying and on her way into the hallway, studiously ignoring the sulking Prima Donna in the dog basket. Sadie had on a sleeveless white dress, which hung in silky folds from her hips. It was the first time she'd been able to dress up for ages so she was making the most of it and the white contrasted well with her tanned skin. She threw on a dark blue fitted velvet jacket and realised she was dressed to match the colour scheme in her new sitting room. She went out of the front door grinning.

'What are you laughing at?' grumped Em 'We're going to be late.'

'No, we're not, we're going to be horrendously early but I suppose, as we're not driving, we can all have a drink first.'

'That's the idea' replied Em.

'I do wish I could drive' said Meg sadly, 'because as I don't really like alcohol, I could have driven you all there and back.'

'Stop worrying Flithers, just enjoy your orange juices.'

Flithers, thought Sadie, struck again by the funny-sounding name. It sounded like she was a butler or a maidservant.

'Are you going to keep your married name Meg?' The question popped out without being fully formed in her mind and, catching Em's 'look', she wished she could pop it back again. Meg seemed oblivious.

'I hadn't planned to. I hadn't even thought about it. Why, do you think I should change it?'

'I think it's entirely up to you,' said Sadie 'What was your maiden name?'

'Hickinbottom' came the innocent reply.

Em's 'look' intensified and it was only now that Sadie interpreted it. Struck dumb, she could only stare at Em, who came to the rescue.

'You can't change it back,' she said definitively 'You've been Meg Flithers for years and I don't intend to stop calling you that.'

'Yes, okay then,' laughed Meg 'That's fine by me. It hadn't crossed my mind really.'

Sadie mouthed Sorry at a glowering Em and then realised they were turning off into the driveway of Winterhill Manor already. They were picking James up on the way as he was joining them. The taxi drove on past the Lodge though and as Sadie looked back, Em told her that James had asked them to pick him up from the Manor itself as there were a few things there he was checking on.

It was a beautiful Summer's evening and Sadie admired the manicured grounds with Em's wonderful fairy statue, silhouetted against the sky.

'It's beautiful Em' she breathed 'as delicate as a cobweb.'

Em smiled to herself as both she and Meg got out. She wouldn't let on but she was quite pleased with it herself now.

'Come on' she said 'Let's have a quick look at the Manor while we're here.'

'What happened to this rush we were in?' moaned Sadie as she followed them up to the Manor.

It was a romantic Jacobean building and the mellow stone lit up in the evening sun, making it seem like something out of a fairy tale. They went through the huge oak door and into the wood-panelled hallway, their footsteps echoing on the original black and white floor tiles. Em headed towards a door at the right and Sadie followed her into a room with deep red walls and...

'SURPRISE!' came a united shout, the loudest shout of all being unmistakeably Ali's. What was she doing here? And Sadie could see her husband George too!

'Wha – what's happening? Have I been celebrating my birthday on the wrong day all these years?' gasped Sadie in astonishment.

She took in the scene before her in a daze. Ali and George were there, she wasn't dreaming. So were Thomas and Joanna, and at the far end of the long dining table stood James. Raff was standing next to him and looking straight at her. Sadie swallowed hard and James came towards her, handing her a glass.

'To our Sadie' his usually gentle voice carrying across the room 'and her new home. Welcome to Brytherstone, where your aunt and the rest of us – feel you belong. '

He raised his glass and everyone made a toast to her and her new home. She could feel her face puckering up to cry. No, she must not cry in front of Raff, she looked so ugly when she cried. Why did that matter? However, she felt a rogue tear betray her by rolling down her cheek very obviously.

'Oh, this is so (sniff) kind of you. Who wouldn't want to belong (sniff) to a village community as kind and lovely as this one is? She raised her glass high in the air, 'To all of you – to my friends.'

They all drank again and Sadie heard a small sob from somewhere to her left and turned to see Em holding a handkerchief to her eyes.

'Emma Norwood! I don't believe I've ever seen you cry!' said James in a bemused voice.

'I'm not crying, Meg's perfume's too strong' Em deadpanned.

'But I haven't got any on?' said Meg and only realised her mistake when people started laughing.

'Anyway, I believe a tear or two might have escaped the other day as well' said Em, recovering quickly and that was the cue for excited explanations about the Dovecote and questions about how Acorn Cottage was coming along – and for Ali and George to join in with their plans. The discussions lasted all through the dinner, words tumbling out from all present.

*

Sadie leant against the chair back and realised she could hardly move from all the food she had eaten. James had placed her at the head of the table and the rest of them were seated down each side of the beautifully set table. He had asked the kitchen staff to stay behind – for a generous financial bonus- to cook a meal for them. There had been a light spring vegetable soup then salmon and spinach with tartare cream, followed by honey-glazed pork with dauphinoise potatoes and seasonal veg. It had been finished off nicely by a French strawberry tart, which, incredibly, everyone made room for. There were now a selection of cheeses on the board and everyone was on to the port, including the women. This *was* the twenty-first century after all. She had drunk at least three large glasses of champagne, which might have been a conservative estimate -

and was on her second glass of port, which she knew she shouldn't be drinking this fast but she was feeling very mellow.

Ali had surprised them all. When she had come up to Harrogate 'on business' and stayed with Em and Sadie, she had been testing the property market around there. She hadn't wanted them to know until it was finalised but…

'George has got a partnership in a practice in Harrogate!' she had squealed loudly, jumping up and down in her seat like a toddler needing the loo 'We've got a lovely big house in a village with a big garden for the same price as the small one in London with a small courtyard. I'll be able to see you ALL THE TIME Sadie!'

Ali had reached a crescendo of which only Ali was capable and everyone had laughed and congratulated them too. There had been a lot of keeping secrets and buying of houses but now it seemed everything was set on a course for happy times.

Sadie felt very content. She sighed happily as she reached out to pour another glass of port. Em, who was next to her, gave her a warning look but Sadie countered it with an 'I'll be fine' look so Em turned and resumed her conversation with Meg across the table. She watched them for a few seconds and then watched James, at the far end of the table. He was in conversation with Joanna next to him but his eyes kept drifting up towards Em. She wouldn't normally have thought too much about it but after Raff's disclosure, she was definitely reading more into it now. She turned towards Raff who was somehow seated at her left; he had obviously followed her eyes and allowed a little smile to pass between them. He held his glass up in salutation and held her gaze for just that little bit too long. She felt as though she'd stopped breathing but then George asked how many people she'd got for the courtyard units and the spell was broken.

Her eyes seemed to go in and out of focus as she was talking to George – she must visit an opticians, there was obviously something wrong with her eyesight. She was laughing at something he had said, what was it now? Her brain seemed to have gone into retrograde motion all of a sudden- maybe she was tired? She suddenly became aware of some of the others at the table waiting with expectant grins on their faces.

'Sorry, I didn't catch that, what did you say?'

'I just asked what you were going to do with the garden. We walked up to your cottage this afternoon from the pub where we're staying and had a look around, Hope you don't mind?' asked George.

Course not, you're welcome anytime. And the garden- I have plans.' She grinned and wiggled her eyebrows.

'Oh no, it's Secret Squirrel time again.' laughed Ali.

'You can talk, with your secret military manoeuvres to Harrogate.' Sadie laughed, aware now that the alcohol was definitely working. 'but no, if you're sitting comfortably, I will begin to tell the tale. You might have noticed just a little way below the terrace, past the grassed area, is what I think was a knot garden with crossed paths and sectioned-off parts?' There was a murmur of assent while she took another rather large gulp of the excellent port.

'Well, I think it was probably a herb garden, maybe started by Agnes Norwood centuries ago. She could have grown the herbs there for her medicinal remedies – or spells as the locals called them.'

Everyone chuckled at this and she could hear Meg explaining to George who obviously hadn't been told the whole story.

'So, I'm going to reinstate it to its full glory and grow all sorts of medicinal herbs in it. Thanks to James who has given me the name of his gardener Ned- who has retired from the estate but not from James. And me – er, - I, whatever, he is going to help me with it as he knows all about herbs and knot gardens.'

'Brilliant idea Sadie.' said Em enthusiastically 'In remembrance of your ancestors – a sort of homage.'

Sadie nodded and looked pleased. She picked up her glass again but was surprised to find it empty. Strange. Had she drunk that much?

'Not only that,' Sadie continued, on a roll now, 'I'm thinking of taking one of the courtyard units myself and selling homemade herb-based products.'

'Wow Sadie – you go girl!' shouted Ali 'You can be a witch too!'

There was laughter around the table again and this seemed to be the signal for everyone to conduct their own conversations about witches, with Thomas holding forth on his discoveries of the history of the Norwoods. Ali though hadn't finished yet. She leaned across Thomas and asked Sadie what she was going to do with the Gypsy caravan at the top of the garden. Sadie was on such a high with all the enthusiasm over her plans that she just said the first thing that came into her head.

'Well Raff here is going to restore it so maybe when he's finished, we could create a path up to it by the side of the field and have it on display?' she glanced at Raff next to her as she said this but was too carried away to notice the look in his eyes.

'We could maybe sell some posies from it or bunches of lavender' she kept on like a runaway train.

'Ooh, buy my lucky lavender dearie!' laughed Ali, who had matched Sadie drink for drink.

Sadie threw her head back and laughed the wild laugh of the truly inebriated who finds everything hysterically funny. While she could hear Ali and George's delight at this not altogether serious turn of events, she was also aware of a strange undercurrent – a cutting silence. Most of them were still chatting about witches but when she turned to Raff she saw his head was lowered and he was staring at a fixed point on the table. Baffled, Sadie looked at Em, sitting opposite Raff. Em sighed, untwisted the napkin she had been holding tightly and said,

'Well, that meal was absolutely beautiful, thank you so much James for arranging it.'

'Yes, you're a star James,' added Sadie in a shaky voice as everyone concurred and congratulated James.

She noticed Raff didn't join in. She turned to him again and he met her eyes but it wasn't the playful look of earlier. His eyes were narrowed, his mouth was set hard and distaste was written all over his face. She only just had time to register that when Raff scraped his chair back.

'Have to go' he mumbled up towards James who had to lean forward to catch it. 'Early start tomorrow' and as James put his hand up in salute, Raff walked resolutely past Sadie and out of the door without saying a word to her.

People were saying their goodbyes to each other but Sadie just stared at the door uncomprehendingly, then turned back and caught Em's eye. She could feel tears pricking her eyes. She wanted to run after him and ask him what his problem was. She wanted the ground to open up and swallow her. She never wanted to see him again. She never wanted to see alcohol again. All these thoughts chased round Sadie's brain but in the end, she leant across to Em and whispered,

'But what did I do?'.

Chapter 21

They were all seated in the corner of the Falling Stone Inn. Em and James had a coffee in front of them as Meg had fed them earlier. Ali and George had just eaten a carb-full breakfast at the Inn and Sadie nibbled morosely at a bag of crisps. George was on bottled water because he was driving back. Ali and Sadie were on bottled water because they couldn't face anything else after the excesses of the night before.

Sadie was thinking about last night. She had waited until they'd got home and Meg had gone to bed before she burst into tears.

'Why did he storm off?' she whined at Em, repeating the mantra for the tenth time slurring her words because the fresh air outside Winterhill Manor had hit her like a brick.

'Possibly because you more or less said you were going to take over his caravan?' smiled Em while she made a coffee accompanied by a pint of water, which she set down in front of Sadie.

'But I can't even remember what I said. And I'm not going to do anything with the stupid caravan. I just said the first thing that popped into my head.' Sadie wailed.

'Aided and abetted by volumes of champagne and port. You and Ali were also making fun of Gypsies and their lucky lavender. That must have stung him?' she said it kindly but Em thought Sadie had to remember because she really needed to apologise and if she couldn't remember what she said, there was no chance of it.

'I didn't say that did I?' said Sadie, horrified, even in her drunken state. I can't believe I said that!'

'No you didn't, Ali did and I don't believe she realised what she was saying either, she was in a worse state than you. You did laugh like a drain when she said it though.'

Sadie groaned and put her head in her hands but her elbows slipped off her knees and she plunged forward. Em looked heavenward and helped her up.

'Come on, time for bed' and she helped Sadie up both sets of stairs with one hand whilst precariously balancing the large glass of water in the other.

*

Now though, Sadie came round to the noise of the Inn and a discussion of last night that she really didn't want to continue.

'Oh god, I really didn't mean to insult Raff' said Ali 'I didn't really think what I was saying.'

'You didn't really *know* what you were saying Ali. I'm sure Raff understood that you didn't mean anything by it' said the loyal George to his wife.

'I'm sure he won't blame you Ali, he'll blame me as always.' sulked Sadie. 'I don't know why he's so hung up about that old caravan. Why was he so offended about any plans for it, even though I haven't really got any? I wouldn't do anything with his stupid caravan and he should know that. Why is it so desperately important to him?'

'That's something you'll have to ask Raff himself, Sadie.'

'You're my aunt, you can tell me, you're supposed to be on my side'

'I'm always on your side, you know that but it's just not my story to tell.'

'Ah, there is a story then?' jumped in Ali.

'Even if there is, I'm not sure I'm going to find out as I might not speak to him again' Sadie sniffed imperiously.

Em sighed. Sadie was a lovely, kind girl with a sunny disposition but there were times, this being one of them, that she was adept at the art of cutting off your nose to spite your face. Em knew all about this, she was the Grand Master at it. James had asked her to marry him a few times since his wife had died five years ago but Em mulishly refused him. There was no rhyme or reason to it, she knew. It was too late to have principles now; those should have come into play when she was having a passionate affair for two years with James while his wife was still alive. The fact that his wife was embarked on a blatantly public affair with someone else at the time didn't make it any better. The affair ended when Inga became ill and died a year later – James nursing her to the end out of an inbred sense of duty, though she led him a dog's life, even from the confines of her bed, towards the end.

Em thought that if she wasn't committed as much to the concept of freedom, James would have had an easier time of it. How could she condemn Sadie for her stubbornness regarding Raff when her own stubbornness perhaps stopped her last chance of happiness? Why didn't she marry the man? She knew why – she was scared to give herself up to one man, albeit the same wonderful caring man, in case it all went wrong again. Her heart had been broken and was still very tender, many years later. She came out of her reverie to find Sadie staring at her.

'What?' she asked belligerently.

Sadie drew back in mock fear.

'I only said that you didn't believe our family were witches.' she laughed, coming round slightly.

'It depends how you would term witches.' Em replied matter of factly.

Sadie gaped, along with the others who she had just been telling about Em's total lack of belief in anything supernatural. She gave Em a lift of the eyebrows conveying the word 'What?', so Em went on.

'I don't believe in witches in the way that Matthew Hopkins and his ilk thought of them in the mid-17th century, when he and others put around 500 innocent women to death. I believe in them as wise women who knew the ways of the land and of nature and had skills passed down to them by generations of healers. They were the first doctors and saved many lives with their herb and nature-based remedies.'

'Ah yes. Agnes saved an ancestor of mine and nearly got put to death because of it!' James explained to Ali and George.

'But there's more to it than that' said Em, as Sadie's eyes widened in surprise. ' I believe our family has a kind of second sight – much diluted over the years until it's nothing more than strong intuition now, which many people can claim anyway today. Centuries ago though, when people were closer to nature and relied on their own wits more, I think that second sight may have been a stronger attribute. They weren't only called wise women for their healing. People went to them for advice and they gave it with more than a little foresight. There's nothing spooky about it – we just relied on our senses more then, things that are taken away from us now more and more, as machines are doing our thinking for us'

'Wow!' said James with feeling.

'Em!' gasped Sadie 'I didn't know you felt like that. Have you been reading Thomas's new book? '

'No, he came to me for information. I'm not quite as anti-history as you might think, there's a lot you don't know about me' she said.

'Are you really a witch then Em?' whispered Ali in mock reverence.

'I have been known for it over the years. Oh sorry, I thought you said bitch.' smiled Em innocently.

That broke the spell that had been cast over them, so to speak, and they all laughed then George went upstairs to get their cases. Sadie and Ali hugged and promised regular phone catch-ups before they lived in the same county. James leaned across to Em.

'You know you're not a bitch, although for some reason you like to perpetuate that myth' he whispered in her ear. 'You're as soft as butter really.'

'Shh' Em whispered back 'Don't let everyone know, 'I've got a reputation to keep up'

*

As soon as they had waved Ali and George off, Sadie and Em walked back down to Church View and Sadie disappeared upstairs to her room.

She came down ten minutes later and grabbed an unprepared Whisky's lead. After the initial shock, Whisky's expression said 'At last, left at home for twenty-four hours and now – Freedom!'

'Just off to check on Acorn Cottage' shouted Sadie.

'No need to shout, I'm just here' laughed Em from the kitchen doorway and pointed at an envelope in Sadie's hand, 'What's that?'

Sadie looked furtive and stuffed the envelope and the roll of sellotape in her pocket.

'Nothing,' she said quietly.

'Of course' Em breathed out slowly through her nostrils.

Sadie, pulled by a jaunty Whisky, opened the front door.

'Don't forget, if you're going to see Raff, he's away for a few days.'

'I'm not.' came the decidedly grumpy reply as the door banged shut behind her.

If I had been one of my ancestors, I would have given her a calming herbal tea, thought Em as she headed for the workshop where Sadie's present beckoned. Good time to get on with it while she was out. There was a sponge cake on the side, left out by Meg, who was doing her

Sunday visiting duties to some of the older Brytherstone residents. Em started to put it back in the tin but decided to go for a knife first. Then she went into the workshop, ready for the creative process, with crumbs all around her mouth.

Chapter 22

Marching down the garden, she stopped briefly to pick some green leaves sprouting at the edge of the herb garden. Should she, or shouldn't she? She decided it was worth a try and put a sprig of the basil in her envelope. She had worked herself up in case she saw Raff again but Em had reminded her he was away, seeing about a commission up in Edinburgh for one of the churches. She turned into the clearing and saw the caravan was standing there with an abandoned air- no woodworking tools, paint tins or open doors anywhere - or any sign of Raff. She breathed a sigh of relief but still listened for Bran's bark, which always heralded Raff's appearance, but there was nothing this Sunday afternoon except for the birds singing and distant, occasional traffic noise on the road to the village.

She looked down at Whisky who was waiting in vain for his new friend. Whisky loved it up here and there was lots of space for him to run around in. She wondered if he'd like to take up permanent residence with her but that might be unfair on him and Em, who actually thought the world of each other.

Walking gingerly up to the caravan, she hesitated a moment before setting her mouth and then sellotaping the envelope with Raff's name on it on the glass of the caravan door. She was about to step back when she had an urge to look inside again. It had been fascinating to see the ornate decoration on the wooden ceiling and she just wanted one more look. She was on her tiptoes when she became aware of a prickly, warning feeling down her back, which made her catch her breath. She turned slowly round to her left to see Raff standing in his entrance to the clearing, two treacherously quiet dogs in front of him, licking each other's ears.

'Checking your property over are you?' came the caustic announcement.

Where Sadie had at first felt embarrassed at being caught out, she now saw red.

'If you'd waited, I'd have apologised but you went off in a massive sulk which was a ridiculously childish thing to do. You could have just told me what was wrong without all the dramatics' Oh God, her mouth was saying all the wrong things. Again.

Raff's eyes narrowed until they were two icy slits of blue under black, scowling brows.

'I went off because, like I believe I mentioned, I had to travel up to Edinburgh at an ungodly hour this morning.' This wasn't all of the truth and they both knew it.

'Well why are you still here then?'

'There was a message on my phone when I switched it back on. His wife's in hospital.'

'Oh, I'm sorry.'

'Don't be, she's just had a little boy and he's just rearranged for another day.'

He looked up and saw the note on the door. He scowled back at her as he tore it off and shoved it roughly in his pocket.

'I suppose that's my eviction notice, telling me you want me and the caravan off your land?' he gestured expansively at the small clearing and then brought his hand back to pat the note in his pocket, 'or did you want me to leave the caravan here so you can sell your herbs and bunches of lucky lavender from it?'

Raff's lips curled in anger as he spat the last words out.

Sadie was angry at his savage attitude but she faced him down. They were like two gladiators at the Colosseum.

'You're just denigrating my heritage, making it into a laughing stock.' Raff's jaws were twitching and his fists were clenched in anger but Sadie's anger was matching it now.

'I am doing no such thing. I respect your heritage and I don't know why you're being so touchy about it anyway. It's pathetic.'

'You want to turn a large part of my forebear's history into a flower shop for everybody to gawp at. You might as well set me up as a fortune-teller while you're at it! If only you knew about the history of this vardo, you would know why I'm touchy about it being turned into a sideshow.'

'I was drunk – okay! I didn't mean to put you or anybody down or laugh at you. I'd just had too much to drink and I said the first thing that entered my head. Happy now? And that's just it, isn't it? I *don't* know the history do I? You said you'd tell me and you didn't.'

'Oh it's my fault now is it?' his voice was a little quieter now, thrown by her confession.

'You were the one who went home before I had a chance to tell you.'

'I came home because I'd been choking on your stupid apple!' screamed Sadie, stung by the unfairness.

There was a pause where they just stared at each other but the longer it went on, Sadie could feel her shoulders dropping, her anger subsiding. As she began to drop her eyes away from his, she just caught the corner of Raff's mouth twitching.

'*Your* stupid apple' he said quietly with the ghost of a smile then he shook his head and closed his eyes. 'This is no good.'

He threw himself on the steps of the caravan, his long legs reaching the floor. He squinted at her through the sun and patted the step next to him. Sadie was thrown momentarily but then hesitantly walked across and sat as far to the side of the steps as she could so she just managed not to come in contact with his body.

She turned to say something but he was leaning back with his head against the door, his eyes closed as if he were exhausted. He looked in pain but Sadie guessed it was because he'd lost his temper and was ashamed, rather than any physical pain. While his eyes remained closed, she took the opportunity to really look at him.

His hair, black as midnight, hung down over his forehead and curled over his collar at the back, almost touching his shoulders. He had a day's growth of dark stubble emphasising his chiselled jaw and pale lips. Those lips, sensuous and turning up almost imperceptibly at the corners, were slightly open, showing even white teeth. His brows were thick and black, his eyelashes too. Sadie would have killed for eyelashes like those. His cheekbones were finely carved and …

'Are you watching me?' he asked, causing her to jump and making her cheeks flush hotly.

'I was waiting for you to say something' she ad-libbed very badly 'Anyway, how did you know?'

'Second sight, all us gypsies have it,' he opened his eyes and Sadie was relieved to see the humour in them, 'and I could feel your breath on my cheek.'

He laughed and she grinned back – all the fight gone out of her.

'I'm sorry' he said unexpectedly, in a low voice 'I *was* touchy and I *did* overreact.'

'And I'm sorry too' she replied with feeling, 'You may not believe this but I actually had no intention of using your caravan for anything. The thought had never entered my head. I just got carried away on a wave of the acclaim of the others, misplaced enthusiasm and too much strong alcohol.'

He smiled at her gently, something indefinable in his eyes and she melted, slowly. She would slide off the steps in a pool of ecstasy if he didn't stop.

'Well,' she almost shouted, jumping up 'I'd better get back because, yes, because I'm not sure if Em will be expecting me back. And Whisky. Expecting both of us back.' Oh god, she was rambling and they both knew it.

Raff unfolded himself from the steps and faced her.

'Maybe you can come to my cabin another time and I'll try once more, to explain the Maguire/Norwood/Bruce history?'

'Bruce? Oh, alright then, I'd like that.' she said.

Raff patted the pocket containing the envelope.

'Do I really want to open this?' He looked down at her with a worried expression.

'I think you will' said Sadie, smiling.

As he opened it, the sweet basil leaves fell out. He rolled it between his fingers and thumb then swallowed hard.

'According to Agnes's Book of Healing, it means 'sorry' or 'forgiveness'.'

'I know what it means' he whispered 'and thank you – but with it, I'm asking your forgiveness too.'

'You have it' she smiled happily.

He read the note inside. 'Raff, you know the caravan is yours, always has been, always will be. It was a bad, drunken joke, just please forget it – and no slur at all was intended on your heritage, which I respect greatly. I am giving you the land it stands on, to go with it, as it should be. We'll get it drawn up legally. Sadie. '

He looked up at her, his brows knit together.

'Sadie, that is a lovely thing for you to do but I don't want the land because it isn't 'as it should be.'

Sadie looked disappointed so he went on.

'This is how it has always been, it would change things if...' he sighed, trying to find an adequate explanation 'Look, wait till Saturday after next, 7pm. Okay? I'm in Edinburgh next weekend. Then I will reveal all.'

He gave a suggestive wiggle of his eyebrows, which made Sadie laugh, and then suddenly, he put his hand at the side of her head and pulled her towards him.

'Sadie, thank you.' he whispered, so low she could hardly hear but that might have been because of the drumming in her ears, which was coming to a crescendo. She could feel his breath on her; his eyes were on her lips. She could feel him pulling closer and she was giving in to the warm, fuzzy feeling that was coming over her.

'Yap!'

'What the?' she breathed, vaguely noticing a small, inquisitive Whisky at their feet, looking from one to the other.

'Where the hell did he come from?' said Raff, looking amused but was there a touch of disappointment there?

'Well,' said Sadie shyly, 'I'd better be off.' The moment had gone and it would be too embarrassing to stay now. 'I'll see you on that Saturday?'

Sadie backed away.

'Don't eat before, I'll cook your dinner' he said.

'No apples' she grinned, looking back to see him laughing as he turned back towards his cabin.

She and Whisky walked back up the garden, Sadie with a ridiculous smile on her face and Whisky with a look of 'mischief accomplished' on his. Sadie waited till she was halfway down the driveway before she bent down to put the lead on him. She eyeballed him until his eyes stopped trying to avoid her and he reluctantly looked back at her.

'You and I, young fella-me-dog, are going to have to have a serious talk about your atrocious sense of timing.'

Whisky stuck his ears up, which perfected his 'Who, me?' expression.

Chapter 23

Sadie's excitement was palpable. She was buzzing and anxious at the same time. She had spent all morning up at the house after the cleaners had finished their second marathon house- clean the day before. This time they were cleaning up after the painters and carpenters had finished. She now went from room to room hugging herself as though she had received the best present ever from Santa. Which she had, although Santa couldn't claim this success from her really as she had planned, bought, planned again, chosen and supervised (with help from James and Em) the whole thing herself. She was so pleased about it that she was willing to believe in the tooth fairy, the Easter bunny and Santa too. Oh Christmas… she thought, wouldn't it be wonderful at this place, so perfect for it?

She checked the kitchen, the large scrubbed pine table could accommodate twelve people at least and the place was so cosy now. The Aga gleamed and the light poured in. The white - or 'apple white' apparently - units went perfectly with the slightly darker sage green walls. It had retained its farmhouse style but had a fresh, modern feel to it too, which Sadie felt went well in a kitchen. The French doors were open to the terrace to get rid of the lemony cleaning smell left behind although Sadie actually liked it- it added to the newness of everything.

She looked up at the ceiling. Holly and ivy could be pinned along the beams and the tree…ah, where would the Christmas tree go? She wandered into the hall – it was large but not large enough for the tree she had in mind. She looked in on her study, which overlooked the front garden. The pretty, cottagey wallpaper had small sprigs of lavender on which reminded her of 30s-style wallpaper. It was purely her choice although it didn't go with the rest of the house. It was perhaps a subconscious homage to the great-gran she never knew and it made her feel safe, somehow. It would be so relaxing working in here, working out what herbal gifts to sell in her shop unit and, although it hadn't formulated properly in her mind, she wanted to write a book about the family she had just discovered.

Across the hall and with its wonderful window-seat looking out over the front was the sitting room. It was done out exactly as she had envisaged it, in dark blue and cream with a midnight blue suite and a cream carpet. Sadie grimaced at the thought of keeping it clean but she imagined that she, and any visitors, would be spending most of the time in her welcoming kitchen anyway. This room would be like the parlour of her great-gran's time, kept for best and for when she wanted to watch TV on an evening.

Back down the hall again, on the opposite side to the kitchen, she came to the dining room. In measurement, it wasn't quite as large as the kitchen or the sitting room but it appeared to be just as big because of the lack of objects in it. It had a solid oak dining table in it that her parents had bought. Not personally of course but they had sent the money for her to buy something for the house – so she had asked when she last rang (why was it always her?) if she could buy a table with it. They said yes while being totally uninterested in what kind of table or indeed in the old family house itself. She thought Em had been right and her mother just wanted to distance herself from her unconventional ancestry. The money had run to a matching dresser along the side wall too, the one opposite the fireplace. Her eyes alighted on the far, right-hand corner, away from the window. That was it! She had found the place for her Christmas tree. The table was still large enough to seat plenty people and Christmas dinner would be better in here anyway, away from the smells and clatter of cooking. There was still that lovely view down the back garden and beyond to the fields through the French windows – slightly smaller than those in the kitchen but still big enough.

Her expression dimmed for a minute. She was building herself up for an event months away and the odds were that no one would want to eat here. After all, they'd managed perfectly well without her and Acorn Cottage for years before she came. Ali would be in her new home. Maybe Em and Meg? What about Raff...?

She told herself off sternly, nothing was going to spoil today. The first people were coming to view the units, although there were only three of the eight left now. There was one for herself with her herbs, Joanna and her friend with knitting and small felt-craft gifts, Meg with her baking, a friend of Em's with stained-glass gifts and

Shelley Cobb, the landlord's daughter who made lovely jewellery in her spare time.

She looked at her watch; she would just have time for a quick sandwich, supplied this morning by Meg and now in the brand new fridge. She opened the fridge door to retrieve it and made a mental note to get some supplies in for when she came up here. It would be a couple of weeks yet until she officially moved in. She looked warily at the Aga – she had always wanted an Aga but hadn't a clue how to cook on one. That would be interesting. She hoped the house insurance would cover her learning attempts. Meg had said she would love to use it, she was brought up with one so in that case it would be well used.

Finishing off the cheese and salad sandwich while walking towards the front door, she reflected on how perfect her new/old house was to her. Repairs finished, decorating done, floors treated or carpeted, window shutters working and all the furniture in place - all in record time. The bathroom was still a work in progress but that too wouldn't be long. It had all gone like clockwork, largely due to James and his unofficial project managing and Em's chivvying. She hoped that this afternoon's transactions would go as smoothly.

Chapter 24

'Oh dear, didn't it go well?' asked Meg with a worried frown on her face. She had put the kettle on as soon as she saw Sadie flop into the armchair, looking like she was in need of a pick-me-up. Sadie opened one eye gingerly then closed it again.

'Everything is fantastic Meg. I now have all eight of the units rented out. The people who came this afternoon were really nice.' She yawned and stretched. 'I'm just so shattered. It's just been non-stop for nearly three months now and I can't seem to come down from 80mph. My brain has been jumping about like a flea on a dog. Now everything is more or less done, the tiredness is overwhelming me. My brain's tired.

It's like someone has given me a sedative that's knocked me out.'

'Poor Sadie,' Meg sympathised, 'You're just like Em though, you never appear to lose your energy.'

'Well I have now' she gratefully took the hot cup of tea Meg gave her. 'Thanks Meg but I think I'll take this to my room and have a lie down before Em gets back and twenty questions start. Where is she by the way? '

'Don't know' answered Meg automatically, 'she went off in the car.'

'Gone to see James then' said Sadie, sleepily. Meg smiled.

'Your brain's not *that* tired then?' she laughed.

Sadie grinned back, found even that was an effort and wearily dragged herself up the stairs to bed.

*

She woke to the tempting smells of Meg's cooking. Although naturally more of a plain cook, she had recently started experimenting a bit more and this smelt like one of those days. It was definitely a spicy smell. She opened one eye to see the clock and realised she'd slept for four solid hours. She'd obviously needed it though and felt rejuvenated. She lay still for a minute and realised her head felt very hot and fuzzy and she wondered if she was starting with a temperature. This chain of thought dispersed as soon as she moved and Whisky jumped down from the pillow above her head.

'How did you get in here, you rascal?' she mock-shouted and took herself and the furry pillow-warmer downstairs.

Opening the kitchen door, she found Em and Meg seated there. It was after 8pm and Sadie felt guilty.

'You haven't waited for me?' she said.

'Course not,' barked Em 'ate ages ago. We're just waiting to find out about the courtyard units.'

'Ah' laughed Sadie, as Meg put a delicious-looking creamy curry and naan bread on the table for her. 'This smells gorgeous.'

'Tastes it too. Come on then.' badgered Em.

'Can I eat first?'

'Can't you talk and eat?'

Sadie gave up and told them the details between mouthfuls.

'The first couple were lovely. Early retirees. He does leathercraft-he brought a lovely bag that I quite fancy - and she does embroidery, pictures, small gifts – so they're sharing one.

The second couple were younger and very easy to get on with. They make things out of wood. Smaller things so I don't think they'll clash with Raff in his workshop at the cabin. They showed me some quite medieval-looking things, bowls and spoons – and Love Spoons. Small boxes and a beautiful writing slope they brought with them which again, I was eyeing up. I must not buy all the unit's goods before they've even opened!

The third is a man on his own, quite shy but his paintings are wonderful. He does commissions and makes his prints into cards to sell too. I think everyone will get on brilliantly.'

'I hope your optimism is well founded but by the sound of it, I think you could be right.' said Em, 'What about the food side, Meg's unit?'

'Well she's obviously selling her cakes, pastries, pies, bread and sandwiches from the unit, permission came through for her to sell cold food, we don't want the bother of meals as such, the regulations are endless on that. Basically, all the food she sells can be eaten outside at the tables and tea, coffee and cold drinks can be served there too. There's room for six tables in that corner. Enough, I reckon because we can squeeze a couple of tables inside the unit against the far wall, in case of bad weather. Any more and everything would be too crowded. Are you happy with that Meg?'

The beam on Meg's face said it all.

'I think a lot of the trade will be people from the village anyway who want proper home-baked produce anyway but it will be nice to have them and the visitors to sit down with a piece of cake too. I lost my bakery but I've gained so much more. I just can't wait to get in. When does it open? I'll have to get everything sorted for then.'

'Erm, well,' Sadie coloured up, 'I've put an advert in the local papers and taken flyers round the shops – and well – ten days' time actually.'

'What?' chorused Meg and Em.

'That's the Grand Opening because I wanted to catch the greater part of the school holidays. Business will be slower after that but at least we will have established ourselves before we start selling Christmassy things. That's why I didn't want to wait till next Spring. All the units can make a decent profit out of Christmas and make things specifically for the season. They mostly have stock they can just move in. Meg is the only one…' she tailed off.

'Talk about throwing everyone in at the deep end' said Em incredulously, then started to laugh at Meg's shocked face. 'It's okay Meg, we'll manage between us.'

'We will Meg, all hands to the deck' enthused Sadie, 'I've already sourced a coffee machine which will save you time, my gift to you – and the newsagent's lad was looking for a part-time job during the holidays so I said I'd ask you if you needed anyone to wait on the tables?'

Meg smiled and relaxed. With these two powerhouses, she knew she would be ready on time, whatever it took.

'We're not a London store Meg' continued Sadie 'where everything is just so. I'd like the atmosphere to be laid back and relaxed, a 'take us as you find us' sort of place.'

'Sounds good to me' said Em, who had always been a 'take me as you find me' sort of person. 'Have you decided on what you're calling it yet? James will need to know if he's going to get the sign made. You mentioned 'The Cattle Shed because of its former use?'

'I'm not sure. I don't know whether people might be put off eating if it was called that? I thought of something local in it, like Mab's Wood Courtyard or Brytherstone Courtyard but they're too wordy. Acorn Courtyard was another but I'm not sure…'

'Mab's Court?' suggested Meg, quietly.

Sadie looked alert. 'Court as in courtyard but also, with Mab being Queen of the Fairies, it could refer to her royal court. I like that Meg. Mab's Court it is.'

Chapter 25

It was a hot, sultry evening and Sadie had picked a pale lemon, thin cotton dress to keep cool. Rummaging through her knicker drawer for something to go with it, as she was determined not to wear white 'virginal' ones again, she suddenly realised what she was doing and slammed the drawer shut. What was she thinking? Why would Raff Maguire ever see her knickers again, no matter what colour they were? Annoyed with herself for this train of thought, she stomped down the stairs, only to turn round and go back to the drawer. Going knickerless might not be a good idea if there were apples to be eaten. She grabbed a pair of lacy lemon ones and stepped into them.

She took the car up to Acorn Cottage and parked it there. She could spend the night there if she wanted to now her bed was made up with brand new bedding, so she didn't have to worry about having one drink too many. Not that she intended to, she wanted to keep her mouth under control this time.

Walking up the garden towards the field path, even the glorious view over the patchwork of fields couldn't distract her. She felt unaccountably nervous - probably worried that she was going to make a fool of herself again. It was getting to be a habit. Meals and Raff seemed to be a lethal combination involving near-fatal occurrences or apparent insults. She would try to control her tongue and her oesophageal reflexes tonight.

At the end of her garden, she turned left into the clearing and saw that the caravan looked different. Coming close, she could see the rotting wood had been replaced and treated, ready to paint and a cracked pane of glass had been replaced. Reaching the top of Mab's Wood and Raff's cabin, there was no Bran to greet her, which was unusual. She knocked loudly on the door but no footsteps, or indeed noise of any kind, could be heard. Sadie looked down at her dress and thought of all the care she'd taken with her appearance tonight – and he'd forgotten!

She mentally went through her last conversation to make sure it wasn't her who had the wrong date or time but no, she knew she had the right Saturday evening. She was just about to turn away, swallowing hard and feeling more disappointed than she would admit, when she heard a rumbling from the farm track at the other side of the strip of woodland. Then Raff's Land Cruiser flung itself into view, scattering stones in its wake.

Raff flew out of the door and shouted,

'Sorry, forgot the wine. Didn't want to give you the homemade stuff again, or anything to do with apples.'

He held a carrier bag up, grinning at her and Sadie felt her shoulders relax as Bran rushed up to greet her.

*

The broccoli and salmon pasta bake was delicious and she was just finishing off the juicy strawberries for afters, when Raff poured her a second glass of wine.

'That will do me tonight thanks.' she said.

'Are you driving?' Raff asked.

'No, I'm staying at Acorn Cottage but I'd rather keep a clear head tonight.'

He looked rueful. 'Look, that was just me being over-sensitive.'

'...and me not being sensitive enough.' replied Sadie as she and Raff smiled at each other. He looked straight into her eyes in such a way that she jumped up in embarrassment.

'I'll help you clear away.' she gulped.

'You're my guest, I'll clear away- just enjoy the evening.' He gestured out to his own orchard garden and beyond that to Mab's wood. The mellow light was still shimmering, casting long shadows on the hills and valley further on. They had eaten on the balcony again, a little breeze making the too-warm evening bearable. She waited for him there, sipping her wine and thanking fate that she had taken the chance to move to this wonderful part of the country. Raff sat down opposite, looking at her quizzically.

'It's so beautiful.' she breathed, by way of explanation.

'It is' he agreed, 'I'm so glad I moved here.'

She turned towards him with a puzzled expression.

'But I thought you were born here?'

'Ah... I think it's time I told you the story, isn't it? he smiled.

Chapter 26

'A long, long time ago' began Raff, in a deep American drawl.

'In a galaxy far, far away' interrupted Sadie, as he had meant her to.

'…there was your great, great grandmother and my great, great, grandfather.'

'Great!' winked Sadie as Raff looked heavenward in mock annoyance.

'Well actually' he continued, 'our families were connected well before then, maybe even back to Agnes. Although way back in the mists of time, the Maguires were from Ireland and could trace their origins to the ancient Kings of Fermanagh. Hence the Celtic looks.'

Raff indicated his very pale blue eyes and his almost black hair and eyebrows.

'We came over here a few hundred years ago or so - I'm not sure when- as Irish gypsies. I don't know what went wrong with the Royal ancestry except to guess that wars, usurpers, traitors, famine and bad luck had a lot to do with it. Anyway, we were penniless and roamed, as was the traveller's custom, up and down the country, with a horse and covered cart and a tent at first until we had the Vardo made. We stayed wherever we could until we were moved on. Every summer though, my family always ended up here, in the clearing, because your family always welcomed them and were happy to let them stay on their farm, even letting us use that small clearing as our own.

A friendship developed between the two families and they always spent a lot of time in each other's company. Especially so, when your great, great grandmother Eliza and my great, great grandfather Sylvanus, fell in love.'

'Ooh, what happened? Did they get together?'

This was a turn-up for the books thought Sadie, who couldn't help another, unhappy thought intruding. Could this mean that she and Raff were related?

'Did they have children?' she continued, warily.

'No, your wicked ancestor was already married and they were into their forties by then anyway. It was an 'affaire d'amour' but it was also a meeting of minds. It continued until he died while on the road one winter. She was heartbroken but carried on her life with her husband and daughter who inherited the farm after they had passed on. Another glass?'

It took Sadie a few seconds to register his last question as she was so entranced by the story. Their families really were connected.

'Oh go on then.' she said as Raff smiled at her faded good intentions. 'Well, I've got to hear the end of the story haven't I?'

'Now to move the connection on through the generations. I am telling you all this as it has been handed down to me. Your great-grandmother and my great-grandfather had been childhood playmates in time snatched during our family's stay here. They spent their summers together, roaming the fields and building dens in Mab's Wood.'

'Just like we used to do!' grinned Sadie and with a jolt, realised that her family was as connected in this generation as in others.

'My grandfather took over the family vardo when his father died and continued the traditional way of life. It all changed when my grandfather fell in love.'

'Not with my grandmother?' asked Sadie, open-mouthed, as she had been quite taken with the grieving war widow story.

'No, of all things, with the daughter of a minor Scottish aristocrat, a member of the ancient Bruce family. There was a substantial Tower house in the Scottish Borders- not a castle by any means but still... Of course, her family disapproved of the match as I suppose they would. We hadn't a penny and they were comfortably off. They wouldn't relent, so she ran away with the gypsies! Although she loved my grandfather and wanted to marry him, she couldn't take to a life on the road. So your grandmother, who had become a good friend to them both, allowed them to pitch the Vardo in the clearing permanently. After my father was born, the Bruce grandfather and his wife died in an accident without ever having made it up with my grandmother Margaret. As she was the only living child, she inherited Broch Tower. With me so far?' Raff grinned as he saw her rapt expression and Sadie nodded impatiently.

'Although the marriage was a happy one and there was no doubt they loved each other,

Raphael, my grandfather found that way of life as alien as Margaret did with the travelling way of life. He didn't take well to being cooped up inside bricks and mortar so came down here as often as he could. Just the fact that he could sit outside on a night, smoking his pipe and being at peace with nature and the stars, revived him for his next round of 'imprisonment' in Scotland.

The whole family, including Margaret, still spent summers here. He instilled in my father Patrick and later me, a love of this caravan and of this small corner of England. Your grandmother offered him the additional strip of land at the top of Mab's Wood and Raphael bought it to build a house on for Margaret but she died before they could ever discuss the building of it.'

'Oh that's so sad' said Sadie 'but at least you built on it in the end.'

'That's what I meant about 'coming to live here'. I was actually born in a small Scottish Tower but, like my father and grandfather, it never felt right. My father spent a lot of his time down here and brought us too. My elder brother, who was much happier with his home life and had never 'got' the holidays in the Vardo, took over the castle when our parents died. I took over this land instead. So, when I used to play with you and the rest of the kids here in Mab's Wood, I was just like you, here for the summer holidays and staying in our old caravan. After my father died, I built the cabin you're sitting in now.'

'Wow' breathed Sadie, settling back against the chair, 'what a story. I can see now exactly how the Norwood and Maguire families are inextricably connected.' Without being related, she thought and found this strangely comforting.

'And maybe you can see now why I was so antagonistic at first, with this 'stranger' trespassing on Norwood land?' he laughed, recalling their first meeting 'I was just protecting the land. Can you also see why the family vardo is so precious to me? I've let it start to decay and I'm ashamed of that fact so I've started restoring it. I need to take care of the vardo that hosted a passionate love affair between our earlier forebears. My grandfather was born in it too, as well as many before him, in that very clearing, so I just couldn't give it up.'

'I understand now. Of course I do, completely.' she replied, 'I can see why you walked out after the dinner that night. Like I've already said and meant, the clearing is yours too. Not just to use but permanently. We can get a solicitor to…'

'No! Don't you see?' interrupted Raff, 'that will break the bond of trust that our families have between them. We have never needed or wanted anything in writing- it is an unspoken contract. It is the friendship between us all and its meaning is so much more than legal contracts or written deeds. Yes, the Vardo is mine but the land is ours.'

'Ours' she whispered, repeating the gentle way he had said the word and then coloured as she realised how intimate it all sounded. She also realised it had become dark as the story had unfolded.

'Thanks for telling me the story Raff and' she peered over the balcony 'I think I'm going to need a torch now and I forgot to bring one.'

'Oh, are you going?' he asked, looking disappointed, 'Yes, I've got one and I'll see you to the cottage.'

Raff rose from his chair and held his hand out to pull her up. For a moment they gazed into each other's eyes as their fingers entwined but Raff moved away quickly to find the torch. Sadie swallowed her disappointment and grabbed her bag.

She asked a few more questions about the past as they went outside but mostly they walked in silence. Sadie felt awkward, as though she had only just met him or like she was on a first date. She immediately swept this last thought out of her mind. It wasn't a date. He had needed to get that story off his chest and she had wanted to hear it. That's all. They reached the light from the coach lamp at the back of the house and he turned to her.

'Are you alright now?' he asked

He wasn't even going to come in for coffee thought Sadie sadly, as though he couldn't wait to get away.

'Yes thank you – and thanks for the meal too-and our family history.'

She couldn't see his expression properly. Just the lamp shining brightly in his eyes and on his parted lips and the fact that he had moved much closer without her realising. She felt his strong hands on the top of her arms, drawing her close, very close. His lips, when they touched hers, sent such a thrill through her body that she could hardly breathe. Her lips pressed into his urgently and she gave into him entirely, her body feeling weightless. After a minute a two, he pulled reluctantly away, stroked the side of her face and whispered gruffly in her ear, 'Goodnight, Sadie Norwood.'

'Goodnight, Raff Maguire' she whispered back and watched his retreating figure until it disappeared into the darkness. Then she turned towards the back door with a silly smile on her face, which didn't disappear until she went to sleep.

Chapter 27

Surveying the finished statue of Gaea, Em reflected on why she had been so determined to create this figure for Sadie and for Acorn Cottage. It somehow seemed more important than it should be. After all, it was only because she was reproducing Sadie's favourite statuette in her bedroom but it had gone beyond that. Her train of thought was interrupted by Meg popping her head round the door.

'Sadie's here to run me and a load of bags and boxes up to the Cottage' she said.

'Oh?' replied Em, absentmindedly.

'You know that I'm doing lots of baking for the opening and she very kindly said I could use her big kitchen?' she reminded Em.

'Oh yes but you know you can use our kitchen anytime you want – you know I never use it.'

Meg looked pleased at the 'our' but Em knew she thought she was in the way, although she wasn't in the slightest.

'Thanks, I know that but because there's so much today – and she has the Aga and the electric range up there too. Plenty storage too until we can take it down to the courtyard.'

'I'll come up later and help' shouted Em as Meg rushed off to Sadie's waiting car.

Em stood back and surveyed the statue. Maybe she'd call for James so they could see exactly where the statue and fountain were going. He and Ned were going to lift it, very carefully she hoped, into the back of her land rover and pad it well in to help her set it up before the moving-in party began. Meg and the Mab's Court gang were under strict instructions to keep Sadie well away from the Cottage until they had all closed their units and made their way to the back garden.

She needed a card first from the newsagent. A New Home card. She was going to write 'Welcome to your New/Old Home which has been waiting for you to reclaim it.' Em smiled and shook her head. She wasn't given to flights of fancy- she was so down to earth that people thought she had no imagination. How you could be a sculptor and have no imagination obviously didn't occur to them. She just didn't let it run away with her and besides, Sadie felt the house calling her and Em had to agree, fate seemed to have intervened an awful lot.

Em held the jeep door open for Whisky, who always liked to be made a fuss of by James. Calling at Pike's newsagent, she chose her card while Whisky sniffed at the dog treats on the counter with a hopeful air and wondered if he'd been good enough to receive one this week. He had his doubts.

Em bought the card and put it in her voluminous smock pocket when she caught sight of something through the window. A breakdown truck was driving slowly past, probably not sure of his way but her eyes moved to the mangled wreck on the back, its driver's side so totally bashed in that it nearly reached the passenger seat. Forgetting everything, she flew outside and screamed like a banshee at the man in the truck.

'The driver, the owner... Where are they? Are they alright?'

The driver gave an apologetic shrug and wished he were a million miles away.

'Where? Where was the accident?' she screamed, wanting to pull him out of the cab and talk sense to her, even if she herself was raving.

He pointed in the direction of the Gressleigh Road before he pulled off again, relieved to escape.

Em shot across the road to her land rover, flung herself in the seat and screeched off towards Gressleigh at twice the speed limit.

'James!' she said out loud, her voice croaky. That was James' car. Nobody could have survived that – or at least not without appalling injuries. She looked out for signs of an ambulance or police presence on the road but there was nothing. Her speed was getting so high now that either there would be another accident or her car would fall apart with the pressure.

Winterhill Manor was coming up. Should she stop there? Or carry on straight to the hospital? Would anyone at the Manor know anything? She made the decision at the last minute and swung into the driveway at 60 mph, sending gravel in all directions. She came to a juddering halt at the end of the Lodge's driveway.

His car wasn't there! She had hoped, blindly as she knew that car well, that the wreck hadn't been his. Now though, its absence from the driveway made it certain. She dropped her head onto the steering wheel. Her hands were shaking, her whole body was shaking, and she didn't think she could drive an inch further.

Gradually she became aware of someone standing at her driver's side window and as she looked up, all the breath was sucked out of her. She tried to say something but it was just a series of gulps.

'Em, what on earth is the matter?' said James anxiously 'Is everyone okay? Are *you* okay? '

She stared at him for a minute, nodded dumbly and to James' consternation, burst out into hysterical laughter.

'Come on' he said, alarmed at her behaviour, 'let's get you inside. Leave the keys in, I'll pull it into my driveway and then make you a cup of tea. Maybe with four sugars?'

He smiled at her and his voice calmed her. She climbed out of the land rover and made her way shakily to the Lodge, sitting on the sofa before her legs gave way. Two minutes later, James was kneeling down in front of her, only pausing to switch the kettle on.

'What's happened Em? Please tell me.' he whispered.

Em stood up and slowly paced up and down before coming to a halt in front of him. The anger came out then, as it always would with Em.

'I thought you were dead! Your car was so badly damaged there was no way you could have survived. Yet here you are, happily making a cup of tea, alive and well!' she shouted accusingly.

James frowned and then realised what had happened. 'You'd rather I was dead?' he tried.

'It's not FUNNY!' she yelled, staring into those oh-so-familiar, kind eyes that she thought she might not see again. Staring until her body went weak, her face crumpled and she did something that worried James more than anything – she burst into tears. Gut-wrenching, heart-rending sobs that just wouldn't stop.

He put his arms round her and held her tight, moving one hand up to her hair and stroking it softly, while talking quietly in her ear.

'I'd parked the car round the back of the Manor, in a stupid place I suppose, looking back. The concrete mixer, which is here for the new staff car park area, was parked there too but no driver. He arrived from the front and didn't see my car behind it, especially as it hadn't been there five minutes before. He jumped in the cab, backed up quickly and – well, you saw the result.

I wasn't even in it Em. I couldn't be angry with him, as I'd parked behind him in a blind spot. He was upset but I told him it was all my fault. It was an accident and I didn't think to let anyone know-let *you* know- as nobody was hurt. The breakdown truck picked it up this morning. I had no idea you'd see it and think....I'm so sorry my darling.'

He squeezed her tightly and listened as her breathing calmed and her sobs subsided. She pulled slightly away from him so she could look into his eyes again.

'You're an idiot, do you know that?' she said shakily.

'Yes, I've been told many times. Mostly by you.' he smiled. 'So – you'd miss me then if I wasn't here?'

'Course I would' she grunted.

'And you've finally realised just how much you love me?'

'Don't push it.' she growled but her eyes smiled.

'Well actually, I thought I would push it and press home my advantage.'

'James,' she started and then paused. She did love this man and she did want to spend the rest of her life with him. She would even marry him because he was wonderfully, gloriously alive. Tears pricked her eyes again as James continued.

'And ask you – again – for the hundredth time, to…'

'Yes.'

'Yes?'

'Yes, I'll marry you, you irritating man.'

'How romantic – and there I was, only going to ask you to make a cup of tea.'

She reached down for a cushion and hit him over the head with it, then hesitated.

'Not really?' she wondered aloud, unsure of herself all of a sudden, in a very un-Em-like way.

'Em! Of course I was asking you to marry me. I thought if you wouldn't now, you never would.'

'That's cruel – and I may change my mind tomorrow.'

'You can't. I'll marry you today. In an hour.' he laughed

Em knew she wouldn't change her mind though. The agony she went through when she thought she'd lost him would always be with her and she couldn't bear the thought of him not being there. She wanted to be with him from now on, more than anything else on earth.

Chapter 28

There were boxes all over the dining room table, mostly laid open with their contents spilling out onto the table and floor. Meg had taken over in the kitchen so Sadie had commandeered the dining room. Herb sachets, herb pillows, herbal creams, herbal teas, herb seeds and separately, over near the window, small pots of living herbs. Herb heaven.

Sadie was pleased with them all. They would fill her small courtyard unit and she had commissioned Drew, their resident artist, to paint some botanical herb paintings both to put on the wall for decoration but also to sell if anyone wanted them. The herb pots she would put outside to tempt them in. She had already bought a small wooden crib stand that the hippie couple, Fran and Col, had made, to put them in.

Of course, she planned to be self-sufficient eventually, when the herb garden was producing enough but for now, she would buy them in. She had already ordered some spicy cinnamon and clove sachets and cinnamon and ginger teas for Christmas.

She repacked the goods to take down to Mab's Court and check on her lists of which she had many. Adverts appearing in the local papers and the Yorkshire Post – check. Invitations all sent out for the opening – check. Homemade fliers sent to the other villagers of Brytherstone courtesy of an obliging – and richer by twenty pounds – paperboy, – check. Invitations sent to all the unit owners and her friends and their families to an informal party in her garden on the evening after the units closed – check.

She so hoped it would be a success although she could feel 'in her bones' that it would be. She had been carried through all of this – the purchase of the property, the plans for Mab's Court – on a wave of euphoria, with the complete optimism that all would be well. She hoped she hadn't set herself up for a fall.

She loaded the boxes into the car to take down and within an hour, everything was laid out on the tables, which were covered in fresh, green gingham. She spent another twenty minutes putting the finishing touches to displays and laying sprigs of fresh herbs between the products then took the car back up to Acorn Cottage.

After checking on a red-faced Meg who was a blur of action between the Aga, the modern range cooker and the large fridge-freezer, she noticed Ned was outside, over near the knot garden, looking very industrious. She went out, watching him hard at work planting up the herbs from pots. She was relieved that James had recommended his own ex-gardener from Winterhill. James had been such a help, as had Ned.

Ned was retired now, ostensibly, but was going crazy at home with only a very small garden to keep him occupied. There were times when Sadie thought she was giving him too much to do as he was no spring chicken but he was as strong as an ox from all his years of labouring outside and he took obvious pleasure in his work. When she had asked him to restore the knot garden and fill it with all the old–fashioned herbs, his beam of delight made her satisfied this was what he wanted to do, rather than 'potter' at home.

He had also asked if he could use a small strip of land at the side of the cottage, near Em's new studio, to grow veg. He would share the produce with Sadie and any surplus they would sell at a stall on the roadside at the front, which would also serve to tempt the customers inside.

As she approached, Ned straightened up and noticed her for the first time. He put his hand up to indicate 'stay there' and hurried off to the stone outhouse he was using as a potting shed and to store his tools. While she waited, bemused, Sadie surveyed the restored knot garden with pleasure. The dwarf box shrubs, which Ned was bringing back to life, ran alongside paths made from old bricks, many of which were found under a good six inches of this soil, in situ. They were set in a herringbone pattern and in the shape of an oddly-formed cross. Ned had wanted it perfectly symmetrical but then agreed with Sadie that, as it seemed to have been laid out that way for hundreds of years, there was no point in changing it. Maybe there was a reason?

Inside the box hedge 'rooms' were lots of newly planted herbs. Sage, Hyssop, Rue, Basil, Lemon Thyme and many others she couldn't recall the names of, although she hoped they would become very familiar. In all four corners were Borage, Feverfew, Chamomile and Dill, then surrounding the outer paths was a wall of Lavender. The whole knot garden extended to at least nine yards by nine – a special number in herb lore according to Agnes in her book, as apparently three times three was a strongly magical number. At intervals, Ned was going to plant nasturtiums, marigolds and more cottage garden flowers to attract the bees. The whole thing would be the focal point of the garden.

The only thing that jarred was the hole in the middle of the knot garden. Ned had hummed and haw-ed at her suggestion of a large Grecian urn (won't go), an ornate sundial (hmm, not sure) and a birdbath (wrong place). Now by the looks of it, he was digging a well, she thought as she peered through hastily pegged in chicken wire covering a deep round hole.

As Ned approached again, she pointed at the hole and was about to ask what he was digging when he said,

'Never mind that. Look here, these are all things I dug up as I was doing the knot garden. Most of 'em, just pieces of pottery and bits of metal, nothing exciting I don't think'

She picked up a piece of the pottery and could see a faint blue and white pattern, probably the ubiquitous Willow Pattern.

'But maybe my family used this, so it's exciting to me.'

'Aye but as I were digging out the…' and he waved in the direction of the hole.

'The well?' grinned Sadie. Ned ignored her.

'I came across this'un. Wiped a bit of the muck off her and –well, I think this metal might be gold.'

Sadie took the object from him. It was a small figure of a woman. She couldn't make out any great detail but there was a broken link at the top, which may have meant it was originally suspended from a chain. She rubbed it and peered closer. It looked as though the figure had long hair and perhaps a cloak or robe. What appeared to be a garland of flowers round her head now sent a tingle down her spine.

'It looks like Gaea, the goddess statue in my bedroom at Em's!'

'Aye, it could well be.' replied Ned, pleased at her obvious glee.

'I must go and show this to Em. Thanks Ned.' she said, bending forward to kiss his whiskery cheek. Ned coloured up, chortled and got back down to his planting.

As Sadie held the figure up to the light to get a better look, the sun blinded her for a couple of seconds but in that time, she had the distinct impression of a woman standing at the other side of the figure she was holding up. The impression of kind smiling eyes looking at her and a mouth curving up in a gentle smile was so strong that she wondered who had found their way to the garden. She stood out of the glare of the sun and there was nothing. She looked all around her, taking deep breaths to try and steady her pulse rate but there was no one here but Ned and herself. Ned didn't seem to have noticed anything- he was setting herbs out.

She blinked and shook her head. Maybe it was a trick of the light but the woman had seemed so real she had expected her to speak. Trying to steady her mind – and her shaking hands – on the way to the car, she reflected that maybe she had been doing too much and needed to rest for a while. It had been pretty full-on what with buying and selling property, starting a business and making her new home habitable. She would have to take it easy. Maybe after the Courtyard Opening?

As she pulled out of the driveway, then into the road leading to Brytherstone, she could see the old tower of the church on the hill, on the outskirts of the village.

'Thomas!' she said out loud. Of course. He knew all about local history and had written a book, newly published, about the early origins of the village. His knowledge of Pagan lore perhaps wouldn't endear him to the Bishop but it could be very useful to her right now, thought Sadie as she pulled up outside the Vicarage.

Chapter 29

Joanna was in the garden deadheading the roses, thick gloves protecting her hands.

'Hello' she called 'Is everything still alright for tomorrow? I'm going up there in an hour to finish setting out.'

'Yes it's fine, going like clockwork. It's just this...' Sadie showed her the little figure, about an inch long and still encrusted with dirt despite its cursory clean, 'and I wondered if Thomas might know something about it?'

'Of course, he'll be in his study. Straight down the passage- door at the end.'

Sadie thanked her then was soon being greeted with a hearty handshake by a beaming Thomas, who was asking to what they owed this pleasure.

'It's your knowledge of early pagans and cults that I'm after – not spiritual enlightenment I'm afraid, that and the history of this village. Have you got time?' she asked, looking at the mountain of books and papers on his desk, although they looked like they'd been there for years and taken root. Thomas looked delighted.

'Sit down, sit down,' he enthused, squinting at the little figure she held out while simultaneously pulling his laptop nearer to him.

'I thought it might be a representation of Gaea,' she explained 'I've had a statue of her at Em's since I was a child.'

Thomas took it from her, peered closely and 'hmmm-ed', then he put on a different pair of spectacles and 'hmmm–ed' again. Then he pulled his spectacle polishing cloth out and rubbed the centre of the figure.

'I can see why you might think that, the average person might' he concluded.

'Are you calling me average' grinned Sadie. Thomas pointedly ignored her and went on.

'But see here.' He pointed out a tiny object the figure was holding in her hands as if it was an offering - and a drape hanging off the back of her shoulders, ending near her feet, 'This all points to the goddess Brighid. The cloak, the flame in her hands – the flowers too.'

'Oh, I didn't even notice she was holding anything. If it is Brighid, what does this flame mean?'

'Well, she is a triple goddess. Celtic in origin. The flame represents dawn but can also represent hearth and home and can be interpreted in either context. She usually wears a cloak like this too, along with the garland of flowers. It's the flame really that distinguishes Brighid from Gaea.' he pronounced Brighid as Brid, with an elongated 'i'. Smiling, he stared closely at her. 'Brighid is known as the goddess of healing.'

Sadie let out an involuntary gasp.

'Healing? That's what Agnes and her descendants did -and probably her ancestors too. They were healers – not witches. That was probably her then, in the garden…' she said the last sentence more to herself but Thomas picked up on it.

'You saw her? Agnes, you mean? Or Brighid?' he looked more excited than confused.

'Oh well, I don't know, I saw something,' she blustered, backpedalling 'or thought I did. Just for a second. I think it's overwork.'

Thomas just asked her to go on.

'Well, I looked up as soon as I had the figure in my hands and the sun sort of blinded me I suppose because I thought I saw a woman looking at me in the middle of this blaze of light. I registered that she had kind, smiling eyes and she had a gentle smile on her face. I didn't take in anything but her face but now I think about it, she could have had a head covering on – white maybe - because I didn't get any impression of her hair. '

'Interesting. Yes, interesting indeed.' mused Thomas. Brighid usually has her hair loose around her shoulders but sometimes you can see her hood. What are your feelings about what happened?'

'You'll think I'm crazy.' Sadie coloured up and stared at the floor.

'I can assure you I won't' said Thomas expectantly.

'Alright. I thought – I felt- that it was Agnes, my ancestor who wrote the Book of Healing we have. I felt - and this is something I am only realising now, that I had been reunited with something that was hers, this figure – and it was connecting us both somehow. I also,' she hesitated 'I also felt that she was giving me her blessing.'

242

They smiled quietly at each other for a few seconds, Sadie was just wondering if he was thinking of an easy way to back out and ring the hospital urgently, when he reached out and put a hand on her shoulder.

'And I think,' he said 'that if that's what you feel, then that's what it was. A strong intuition, a strong *connection* like that, shouldn't be ignored. Her spirit may still be in the place where she was happy and she may be showing that she is happy even now because you, her descendant, are back in the family fold. And Brighid' he held the figure up 'is an amulet, a charm for protection, so she is perhaps letting you know that you are under Brighid's protection as well as her own.'

Sadie stared back at Thomas with his rosy cheeks and wearing his black shirt and dog-collar. Yet, as incongruous as it seemed coming from a vicar, she could absolutely believe everything he said. There were lots of 'maybes' in there but if she kept that in mind, there was no harm in believing what the spiritual leader of her community thought! It all seemed to fall into place and she realised that Thomas's words encapsulated her own thoughts immediately after she had seen the woman. What had seemed like a flight of fantasy caused by a tired mind now seemed much more believable coming from a very grounded and normal person. Besides, her mind wasn't tired at all, she reasoned. It was buzzing with ideas and that was just how she liked it.

'Does your bishop know you're a pagan? Or a druid?' she laughed.

'You know very well I'm not, I'm faithful to the Christian church' he admonished with a grin 'but early Paganism has always been a hobby as it is inextricably linked with the early church, its beginnings and especially its festivals and rites. In addition, being Christian for me doesn't exclude a belief that there are things of this earth that we know nothing about and can't explain logically. Both Christianity and Paganism include a deep spirituality, which is part of the human psyche, and therefore it cannot be separated. So, I conclude my little sermon with an appropriate quote from Hamlet "There are more things in heaven and earth, Horatio, Than are dreamt of in your philosophy." I hope that explains it a little?'

'Thank you for that Thomas' Sadie said, laughing at his self-deprecating note. She wished more sermons could be like that one. 'I'm so glad I came to see you.'

'Just wait a minute' he said, 'and I'll print some stuff off for you. I know all the websites.'

At that moment, Joanna appeared at the door with Raff in tow. Sadie felt rooted to the spot for a few seconds. Why did he have this ridiculous effect on her?

'Come in,' said Thomas, 'we were just looking up the origins of this amulet. Sadie held it up as Thomas turned the screen round to face Raff, who leant down to look at the image there.

'Brig – hid? Brigid? ' he puzzled.

'It's pronounced Breed or more properly, Breej.' laughed Thomas.

'Oh hang on!' said Raff, 'Brighid, the Celtic goddess. I hadn't actually seen it written but my grandfather used to talk about the Celtic gods and goddesses. Our family was originally from Ireland many moons ago and brought their beliefs and culture over here with them.'

He was just gently taking the amulet from Sadie's hands when she squealed; making Raff step back as though he'd burnt her.

'I've just realised' she burst out 'In Agnes's book there are a few spells – I mean potions – for things like Brighid's Balm and Brighid's Poultice. Now I know why.'

'Now, if either of you good people had been to the library and read my new copy of, 'History of Brytherstone', you would know that Brytherstone is a corruption of Bridestone which means Brid's stone. There was supposed to be a standing stone somewhere at the back of where the pub is now but no one has ever found it. Although there is a place on the outskirts called Bride's Well, which was connected to her too. No well there now but it might have dried up or these things might be stories handed down for centuries. It's another thing that links your goddess to the village though.' finished Thomas, grinning like a Cheshire cat. He was in his glory.

'You were meant to come and live here, it really was fate.' said Raff, turning to Sadie. His smile touched his eyes, which were locked onto hers. Then swiftly he pulled back and held the amulet in his hands.

'I came here to see if you needed anything from Gressleigh. For the Courtyard. I saw your car here.' he said by way of embarrassed explanation.

'No, I think we're all good thank you.' she smiled, touched by his offer.

'Perhaps…' he started, 'there's a friend of mine there, a jeweller, who could perhaps clean

Brighid up professionally and find out how old she is?'

'Oh that would be lovely. Thank you again.' then as he started to walk away she shouted 'but you will be careful you don't lose her won't you?'

Sadie groaned inwardly. Why did she have to say that? Now he'd take offence again – he was good at that.

He looked over his shoulder at her, put his hand on his heart and smiled.

'I promise.' he said.

*

After a lot more fetching, carrying, arranging, stressing and rearranging – Sadie finally made it back to Em's where she was going to spend her last night before permanently moving up to Acorn Cottage.

In the hallway, she met with Meg who was just going to take Whisky for a walk around the block as 'he has been in a massive sulk since Em forgot him and left him at the newsagents'. This news perplexed Sadie as firstly, Whisky was now jumping up and down very happily like a puppy on a pogo stick and secondly, Em forget Whisky? Never. She was, admittedly, in another world sometimes but she loved the little rascal and would never have forgotten him. It went out of her mind anyway as she took her jacket off and hung it up as she had so much to tell her aunt.

She began, almost at once, to recount the events of the day to Em, who was sitting very quietly in her chair, for a change. And smiling- also for a change. Sadie told her about Brighid.

'Ah, Brighid.' said Em absent-mindedly.

'So the statue upstairs with the cloak and flowers could be Gaea, like you thought when you made her but more likely, with the addition of a flame in her hands, could also be Brighid. In fact, I'm going to rechristen her Brighid, if you can christen Pagan goddesses in the first place.'

'Yes, not Gaea.' Em smiled placidly 'Name won't make any difference luckily but the flame might. Bit of adjusting. Not too bad.'

Sadie frowned; there was something different about her aunt. She wasn't really making sense and the vitality or even the aggressiveness was missing.

'Are you okay Em?' she asked anxiously 'Only you said you'd be up at Mab's Court later and we didn't see you.'

No.' said Em quietly 'I was …elsewhere.'

Sadie thought that Em was definitely 'elsewhere' now too. She certainly wasn't here.

Sadie didn't like this one bit. She grabbed a bowl of cornflakes for her supper and as she was finishing off, she gazed at Em in concern. Her aunt, who was never still for more than a minute, was just staring ahead unseeing. She couldn't bear it if Em was going senile when she had always been so vital. Poor Em. She put the kettle on then went over and whispered gently in her ear.

'Would you like a nice cup of cocoa before bedtime?'

Em stiffened, put her arms with elbows turned out on the chair sides and slowly turned to face her niece.

'Cocoa? Cocoa!' she spat. 'Have you ever known me to drink cocoa? Are you mistaking me for some old bat who's lost her marbles? What's the matter with you girl? If you must do something, you can pour me a large brandy – and I'm not ready for bed yet! Cocoa…!'

Sadie grinned in relief and bent down to kiss her thankfully still belligerent Aunt Em on the head. It was nice to get shouted at again. Em was back and all was well.

Chapter 30

The sun was already hot even though it was still early morning. Sadie had slept like a log until 4am and had then woken up with a million thoughts in her head. As she looked out of the attic window now, over the rooftops towards the church, she smiled in anticipation of the day ahead. They were opening Mab's Court at 10am. The Grand Opening. It was August 1st, Lammas-tide and she hoped it was a good omen for the fruitfulness of the project.

It was far too early to go to the courtyard. Most of the others were turning up between eight and half past so they could toast each other with a glass of Buck's Fizz and do a last minute check.

She hoped a lot of people would turn up today, not just to have a good nosy around but also to actually buy the products. Most of the tenants though were using their units as a workshop too and at the reasonably low rent Sadie was charging them, it gave them a workshop and retail unit in one. Some of them sold online too- the ones who relied on their crafts as a sole source of income. Others, like Joanna and her friend Betty, were doing it more as a hobby. Sales would always be needed but the secondary use of their units made it more economical and not quite as desperate.

Sadie thought that this aspect would draw the public in as well, an added bonus. Who doesn't like to watch an artist draw his brush across a canvas, marvelling at what object appeared from those few random brush strokes. They could watch designs being punched out onto leather and wooden objects being formed on an old-style lathe, operated by foot. They could watch Joanna knitting her own creations; Betty hand-sewing felt gifts and Shelley Cobb, the pub landlord's daughter, making unique jewellery. Em's friend Artie had a workshop at the back of his house in the village for the larger commissions but would be doing the smaller stained-glass gifts at the unit. The only ones not making anything on the site were herself with the herbal products – but she hoped to change that next year – and Meg, as there were no baking facilities there. Sadie hugged herself and indulged in a self-satisfied grin, which on reflection, may have looked slightly mad to any early dog-walkers looking up at the window.

She went downstairs after a shower and made some toast. Em suddenly emerged from her workroom, locking the door behind her. Watching Sadie's surprised expression at the early hour, Em laughed.

'Just making a few essential adjustments to a commission that's due in soon.'

Sadie nodded. She knew that Em lost herself completely in her work occasionally without knowing what time it was. That was probably what had been wrong with her the night before. She was glad to see her aunt back to normal now.

'I hope you're not too busy to come up to the Grand Opening Em and for a glass of naughty orange juice before it?'

Definitely there for the opening – all finished now.' Em replied, grabbing Sadie's toast and her own land rover keys at the same time. 'Going for James first though, he's going to give me a hand...' she stopped and started again '...with the tables and chairs for the party tonight.'

'Oh, I thought Raff and Thomas were doing them?'

'Yes, well, I thought I'd better direct operations.' she mumbled 'When are you going out of the house? Up there I mean?'

'As soon as I've had some toast if people don't keep pinching it.' said Sadie pointedly. 'Where's Meg?'

'Walked up to the cottage earlier, I gave her my key. She's checking on the baking that's in your fridge and she's going to bake some more. I know you said she could do that at any time so... Honestly, she's so nervous I don't think she'll be able to serve anyone today. '

'Well, it's a good job young Will Pike will be there to give her a hand. I'll be there to give her a hug if she looks like she might hide in a corner somewhere, Don't worry, she'll be fine.'

*

Meg was rushing in and out of Mab's Café with Will following close on her heels. He was trying not to get mown down when she suddenly changed direction, which she did frequently. Sadie had greeted everyone as they arrived but Meg was in a world of her own and Sadie didn't think she had registered her arrival.

'Hi Meg,' she shouted 'come here and have a celebratory glass with us.'

Meg looked like she'd been told that aliens from Venus had landed and were going to make her into marmalade.

'Can't' she squealed 'Got to get all this perfect.'

'Meg, it all looks fine already, honestly.'

'Need to go over it all again' Meg said maniacally.

'For the fifth time...' Will said to Sadie and raised his eyes to heaven.

'I just need to get it, you know – and I haven't finished washing up in your lovely new kitchen. I'm so sorry and there's the party tonight.' Meg looked close to tears.

'Meg, it couldn't matter less, believe me. Anyway, I can slip up at lunchtime and clear up – it's not a problem.'

'Oh would you? Thank you.' said Meg, then... 'NO! You can't. You can't go up there. It will be okay, leave it!'

Sadie stood back in surprise then walked up to put a calming hand on Meg's shoulder.

'Meg, look at me. I won't go up, I'll stay here. Everything will be fine. You've got Will here to help you, it's a beautiful day, so just take a deep breath and relax.'

Sadie left Meg taking that deep breath and with a sympathetic glance at an 'out of his depth with females' Will, she went over to the others. They were gathered in the middle of the courtyard where Drew had placed a table to rest the bottles and glasses on.

She glanced across at her unit, Healing Herbs, and noticed a smart-looking man with a clipboard in his hands, looking through the window. She had an innate mistrust of people with clipboards; it usually spelt trouble. As she watched, he made his way to the next unit, which happened to be Meg's. Oh no, thought Sadie. Confronted by the dreaded clipboard, Meg would fall to pieces. She watched as Meg bustled out and then stopped dead in front of him, her mouth hanging open.

Sadie excused herself and went back to Meg. The man was asking her something about hot food and extractors – and Meg wore the expression of an undersized mouse cornered by an enormous tomcat. As Sadie reached them he was saying, 'If that was the case, then we would have to look into permissions again.'

At that, Meg went strangely silent and then pulled herself up to her full height of five foot two. She thrust her head forward in a threatening pose, fixed her narrow eyes on his and raised her voice to a level Sadie didn't think she was capable of.

'Oh you would, would you? Listen here, Mr. Clipboard, my friend Sadie has been through all of this with your department – with a fine blinking toothcomb. We followed the rules to the letter. She got it all okayed and so we're all ready to open this morning – and open I will! I won't be responsible for my actions if you try and stop me!'

There was a collective intake of breath in the courtyard. Sadie was rooted to the spot with shock. Mr. Clipboard blinked a few times then carried on in the same tone as before.

'But as I was going to say, seeing as that *isn't* the case, everything is fine for the opening.'

Meg blushed from her roots to her heaving chest as the man turned to Sadie.

'Miss Norwood, it's just a routine check before you open. You should have had an email? Anyway, everything seems to be in order.' He looked across the courtyard. 'I'll just go and have a word with Ian, he used to be my boss before he retired and started the leatherwork.'

He smiled at them both in a reasonably pleasant way, considering, then strode across to the middle of the courtyard.

'Oh my goodness' yelped Meg, 'What have I done? He'll close me down.'

'You heard him Meg, it's just routine, everything has passed. I have been so busy I must have missed the email, so I feel responsible in a way. He was only doing his job. Are you okay?' Sadie couldn't help a smile slipping onto her face and when Will came up and said 'You Go Mrs. F.!', she and Will both burst out laughing, leaving a very confused Meg covering her face with her hands. Just then, the clipboard man came back.

'What sort of pies do you make?' he enquired of Meg, with a frown.

The belligerent look had returned to her face.

'Chicken, chicken and ham, steak, meat and potato and vegetable pasties. NOT on the premises!' If she had added 'So there!' at the end it would have been quite in keeping with her tone. Sadie was getting a little worried about being shut down too now. She looked from one to the other as Clipboard man frowned thoughtfully.

'Can you sell me a chicken and ham one for my lunch?' he said finally. 'I know you're not officially open but I have to go now…'

Meg's bottom jaw nearly bounced down to her knees in today's default position and she dashed into the shop, coming out with two pies, one on top of the other, with a piece of carrot cake plonked on the top.

'On the house' she managed to smile weakly.

'Thank you.' the bemused man smiled back.

Sadie breathed a sigh of relief.

'Will you come and have a drink with us?' she offered.

'No thank you, I finish work at noon and I'm driving across to the coast to see my daughter, so I'd better not. Good luck with this endeavour though. It's good to see local crafts being encouraged. Just what we need in rural areas like this.'

With that, he raised the pies and cake to Meg in salute and walked back to his car in the car park. Sadie and Will watched with grins on their faces as Meg ran after him with a slab of fruitcake to take to his daughter.

Em and James had arrived during the blast of invective from Meg and Em was now laughing like a drain at her friend's transformation from mouse to she-wolf. They all, Meg included now, toasted the future success of Mab's Court. Sadie felt sure, as she looked at the smiling faces that this would work, the mix was just right. There was an infectious enthusiasm that ran through them all like an electric current. It also felt very laid-back – apart from Meg's nerves pre-opening nerves- and Sadie could feel they would be a happy bunch of people to work with.

Meg's tables were set up for the free cups of tea and coffee promised for today. Sadie had used this offer to pull the crowds in. Although it didn't seem necessary – at 9.50 am, ten minutes before opening time, the courtyard was packed to capacity. It seemed the whole village had turned out. Not only that-there were lots of people they didn't recognise, drawn in by adverts or word of mouth. They weren't just here for the free cuppas either. They were genuinely interested in the crafts and all the units were kept very busy. People trickled out and others filtered in for the rest of the day and sales were higher than expected. Joanna's friend Betty watched their shop while Joanna gave Meg a hand at lunchtime in case she had another 'moment' but Meg seemed to have worked it out of her system and was now in her element, coping well and smiling benevolently at everyone with no sign at all of her inner tigress.

Chapter 31

The closing time at Mab's Court was officially five pm but at five-thirty, they were still ushering people out of the shops. It had been a very successful day with no lull at all in the amount of visitors. Sadie knew this volume of shoppers wouldn't last but the comments had all been very encouraging. Especially some who said this was the only place to buy proper gifts for birthdays and special occasions for miles around, so they had obviously tapped into a much-needed market.

As the last visitors drifted homeward, all the unit holders began heading towards the garden behind Acorn Cottage, where James, Em and their willing helpers had been getting things ready for Sadie's official housewarming party. She felt blessed to have such good friends. The people she had thought were friends in London, although she had known them a good many years, had been nothing more than acquaintances. She wouldn't have shared a secret with them, possibly more because she knew they wouldn't listen properly. They were always too busy to listen and she realised that now, all apart from Ali, who would always be her greatest and most loyal friend. These people here really cared about others and were willing to help out, even without being asked. She now knew the real meaning of community.

Em had made a couple of trips down to the car park and had disappeared to the Cottage again with some mysterious parcels and all the food accompaniments the Mab's Court gang had insisted on bringing. There were many types of salad: pepper, rice, pasta, tomato, olive and feta, potato and homemade coleslaw - just right for a warm summer's evening. Her parents had sent some money towards the party. Nice of them though Sadie wished she could have said she'd rather see them in person – but she honestly couldn't.

With the money, she had bought some good sparkling wine for the toast plus plenty bottles of wine and beer. Fran and Col were bringing their homemade mead, which Sadie was going to try and keep away from. Last time she had drunk mead, she had danced through the fields at a festival, loudly singing off-key with Ali, like a modern-day nymph without the shepherds. Many of these people lived in the village so could leave their cars here and walk up tomorrow if they wanted to partake of the alcohol.

She had also bought plenty cold meats to serve up on large platters and Em had cooked a lot of chicken pieces in the Aga. Sadie did wonder about their eatability after Em had been let loose on them but pushed that thought aside. She had chopped plenty of veg sticks up the day before and they were all ready in the fridge along with bowls of different dips. There were Meg's crusty breadcakes to eat everything with and some local creamy butter from the farm at the other side of the village, which also provided the cream for the strawberries and bowls of fruit salad. There were platters and boards of various local cheeses from the village delicatessen to finish off with and crispy crackers to accompany them.

Unfortunately, Sadie didn't feel like eating a thing. The excitement of the day hadn't dissolved yet and food was the last thing she wanted. She was just looking forward to thanking all her new friends and neighbours and she hoped this gathering of them all at Acorn Cottage would be the first of many. She felt a warm glow somewhere in the region of her heart just thinking about them and she was sure it wasn't indigestion.

They all made their way to the Cottage en masse and as they walked up the drive at the side, she could hear the others laughing around the back. They were all sitting on the terrace and there was non-stop chatter. Ali and George were there along with their boys, who were running around with Fran and Col's three children and shouts of glee echoed across the fields beyond. Will's parents and younger brother from the newsagent were there as well as Shelley's mum Cynthia from the pub. Jez was still grumpily working behind the bar, despite complaining that half his clientele were at the party anyway.

A cheer went up as Sadie arrived and Ali ran up and hugged her, then stood back to put a blindfold on her.

'Okay, what's this? Blind Man's Bluff? Can we all eat before we play games?' said a bemused Sadie.

'Nope – and careful down these steps' laughed Ali and walking backwards in front of Sadie, took her hands and pulled her along.

Sadie could hear everyone walking alongside her, murmuring and laughing. She could make out the steps below her blindfold and also the legs of the trestle tables, which had been set up on the lawn between the terrace and the knot garden. She noticed she was being guided onto the path edge and could smell the lavender, then they came to a halt.

A silence descended over the guests and as Ali whipped off the blindfold, she could see Em standing directly in front of her looking a little embarrassed. She leant forward to kiss Sadie's cheek.

'My homecoming gift to you, my favourite girl in the whole world. I hope you like her.'

Em stood aside and Sadie's eyes expanded as large as saucers. There in the middle of the knot garden was Brighid. A carved stone Brighid. An exact copy of the one she grew up with in her bedroom in the village. The goddess was standing in the middle of a fountain, a benevolent expression on her face.

'She started out as Gaea but then you realised, thanks to Thomas, that it was actually Brighid.

What I thought was a stone in the old illustrations I took her from originally, was actually a flame. So I've made it into a flame in her hands instead. So, here she is, your own personal protector, for you and the house.'

Sadie could feel everyone holding his or her breath waiting for her response but she couldn't speak. Why couldn't she move? She tried to say something but to her intense embarrassment, it came out as a loud sob. Which was joined by another – and soon she was hugging Em tightly, wetting her shoulder with tears while looking over it at her beautiful statue.

'I love it Em, I absolutely love it! Oh thank you so much, she's perfect.' garbled Sadie.

'Not quite yet, as you'll see.' smiled Em as she extricated herself from the bear-like hug.

Em nodded at James and Ned – and the next moment, the fountain was switched on. The water spouted in a gentle, umbrella-like spray from Brighid's outstretched hands and into the large ornately carved bowl beneath. Everyone applauded.

'You will note that, as Gaea, I made the fountain come through the pyramid-shaped rock she was holding. As Brighid, that rock is now a flame, which makes the water issuing forth a little incongruous. She is a goddess though so maybe it's a miracle?' laughed Em.

Sadie threw her head back and laughed. 'Brighid can do anything she sets her mind to!'

There was general merriment as they all mulled around the trestle tables where James and Raff were uncorking a particularly expensive brand of champagne. Strange, thought Sadie but was distracted by Raff's dark hair curling over the collar of his white shirt and the way his eyes narrowed with mischief when he smiled. However, thought Sadie, snapping back to reality, that really wasn't the sparkling wine that she had bought. James started speaking, his voice carrying easily over to the guests at the back.

'Can I ask you to raise your glasses to our lovely Sadie and to the beautifully restored Acorn Cottage? We wish you all the happiness in the world in your new home.'

'To Sadie and Acorn Cottage.' came the chorus.

'And to the continued success of Mab's Court.'

'Mab's Court.' they all shouted and drained their glasses.

'Before you enjoy the food, if you would like to charge your glasses again,' began James.

There was no problem in getting the guests to comply with his wishes and he and Raff refilled the glasses. Sadie held hers forward although she'd better eat something soon, whether she wanted to or not. She tried to take Em's glass from her for a refill although it was only half gone but Em was grasping on to it and staring at James with a horrified expression on her face. She shook her head at James but he slowly nodded his head at her and smiled. Em turned to a confused Sadie and gave her the glass to top up.

'Now, if everyone is ready' said James. 'I'm sure that Sadie won't mind us hijacking her housewarming?' he looked anxiously at Sadie who inclined her head in puzzled agreement. Of course she wouldn't mind but what on earth was going on? She glanced at Em again who was immobile, her face having taken on a 'startled ferret' look.

'I would like to announce – I am extremely happy to announce, that after countless times of asking - my dear Em has finally consented to marry me. Please raise your glasses to our happiness too.'

There was a moment of complete quiet – then chaos, as everyone tried to congratulate them both at the same time. Many shouts of 'hurrah' and 'about time' were heard from the guests.

Sadie was in tears for the second time today and as James came and put a protective arm around Em, she rushed up to them, putting an arm round each of their necks, nearly strangling them in her eagerness.

'I'm so, so happy for you both, you just go so well together' She stood back suddenly, 'Oh, I haven't bought you anything.'

'And neither should you, we have everything we need at our age,' said Em 'apart from the fact you didn't know as I asked James to keep it a secret. That didn't last long did it?' she laughed fondly at the man next to her, looking into his eyes – and in that moment they were both young again.

Chapter 32

People had eaten their fill of the food and Meg, ever industrious, had cling-filmed the remains and put them in the fridge to bring out later.

Sadie had stood on the terrace wall and thanked everyone profusely. Em and James who she couldn't have managed without, Raff for his expertise with the porch and his help today, Ali for being supportive in everything, Thomas for his history of the house, the unit owners for stepping up and creating the courtyard and the villagers for spreading the word about Mab's Court and coming up to shop. She had paused to see if she'd forgotten anyone and noticed Whisky, looking at her with a hurt expression. 'Oh of course – and Whisky for introducing me to fresh air, exercise and the strange world of eccentric dogs.' Whisky then yapped and ran round in circles while everyone laughed and paid him attention, which he loved.

Music was now starting up as Fran and Col had brought a guitar and a treble recorder and were playing old folk tunes that seemed perfectly in place. Everyone was doing their own version of a folk dance, in a circle and occasionally meeting in the middle like a hokey cokey that had lost its way. The children were spinning each other round so fast that Sadie was sure their supper was going to come back up on the lawn. Whisky and Bran were doing the canine version of a folk dance, which was called 'Go in and out between everyone's legs and see how many you can trip up.'

At the end of one of the dances where she had somehow ended up holding Raff's hand, she made a decision. Keeping tight hold of his hand, she dragged him with her towards the house. He didn't look too upset.

'Come up and see my bedroom.' she whispered suggestively in his ear as they came up to the open French doors.

'Why you forward young hussy!' he shot back in mock horror, then grinned, 'I suppose this is the house tour?'

Sadie laughed and nodded. She had promised him, and Thomas and Joanna, a tour of the rooms, as they hadn't yet seen them. Ali and her family were staying here with her tonight – her first guests – and she needed to show them around too as it was getting late. Sadie knew Ali would want the boys settled in bed before too long so it was now or never.

As they entered the kitchen, they saw Meg making coffee for those who wanted it. She looked a little hyper again but was smiling to herself.

'Meg, you don't have to do that, I'll make them in a few minutes. You're always working.'

'I enjoy doing it. It's what I do, you know that.' replied Meg a little louder than normal.

Sadie had come to realise that it was no good telling her to slow down and she did indeed, look very happy in her task. Her cheeks looked rosier than ever with the champagne she'd drunk.

Sadie looked over to the corner worktop and smiled at the pile of presents. There were carved acorns and scented candles from Fran and Col, framed herb prints from Drew and a bracelet with tiny acorns on from Shelley. Ian's wife Dilly had embroidered a fairy queen for her, complete with crown. No one had come empty-handed. Some of the presents were outside. Apart from Em's wonderful fountain, there was an oak sapling from Ned and James had commissioned Raff to make two signs for outside Mab's Court. Ali and George had bought solar lights on stands, which had been charging up all day along each side of the garden and were now casting a magical light on the garden. Ali knew Sadie loved twinkly lights and had set strings of them in some of the fruit trees too. Meg, as well as making the huge celebration cake in the shape of Acorn Cottage, had bought tea-light lanterns, which were now adorning the tables on the terrace.

She pulled Raff over to the presents and picked up Thomas's present. He had given her a signed copy of his 'History of Brytherstone.' Joanna had made a reed 'Brighid's Cross', both for the housewarming and because it was Lammas Eve and a traditional gift. It had made Sadie gasp as she realised this 'not-quite-symmetrical' cross with the reed knot pulling it slightly off-centre, was exactly the same shape as the crossed paths she had puzzled over in the knot garden.

Raff hadn't bought her anything, which she felt ridiculously disappointed over until she remembered he had carved her the fantastic carved frieze on the porch gable end as her moving-in present. She felt quite ashamed of herself then.

Ali came running in and stopped, out of breath and looked pointedly at Sadie's right hand, which she was surprised to see was still holding Raff's left hand. She dropped it as if she'd been stung and said to Ali,

'Do you want to look around now? '

'Yes please, we saw you coming up to the house and I need to get those boys to bed. All this fresh air will have knocked them out. They'll love life up here in the countryside when we move, we can't wait.' Ali's new house in a village near Harrogate had a large garden for the two boys to vent their energy on, something they had in spades.

'George is staying to watch the boys' continued Ali 'so there's just...and here they are.'

Thomas and Joanna walked into the kitchen bright red and out of breath after a particularly fast dance and so Sadie led the way. They all seemed to love the place almost as much as she did. Ali picked the exact same place for the Christmas tree in the dining room as she had planned herself.

When it came to her bedroom, despite her joke earlier on, she felt quite shy with Raff being there.

'Wow!' said Ali, 'It's Swedish-style but also like the Ice Queen's lair, very clean looking.'

'You like white don't you?' came Raff's amused voice from her side. 'It's very…' Sadie shot him a 'you dare' look, '…very nice.' Raff finished, lifting one eyebrow.

The corners of Sadie's mouth lifted despite herself. As the others filed back downstairs, he pulled her back and bent to whisper in her ear.

'But are you really the ice queen?' and he softly kissed her earlobe, which did unmentionable things to Sadie's body.

Outside, the music and dancing was still going on but a few people were gathering their things together. The Pikes would have to be up early for the newsagents in the morning, it was a bit like Arkwright's shop, it never seemed to close -apart from today obviously. She thanked the departing guests for coming and the willing musicians who would soon have to take their children home. It was still warm and the twinkly lights were shown in full splendour against the darkening sky, which made the garden look like a fairyland.

She glanced at Raff, who hadn't left her side and saw that he seemed far away, his eyes staring into the distance. Suddenly, he grabbed her hand again and putting two champagne glasses in her other hand, he grabbed a bottle of James' good champagne and led her down, past the dancers, to the bottom of the garden.

*

As Raff led Sadie further away from the music and people, he turned to answer the puzzled expression on her face.

'How can you have missed that?' he said, dropping her hand and making an expansive gesture towards the fields and the hills beyond, encompassing a beautiful pink, purple and grey sunset which was turning into a deeper red, moment by moment.

Yes, how could I, she thought. She must remind herself not to get bogged down in the material things in life. Restoring the house and courtyard had brought its own pleasure to her life, but this – the power of nature, the beauty of the countryside and the ability here to see large open skies, went far beyond this. She had forgotten what stars looked like, living in London. Here she would be able to see a star-sprinkled sky, a whole universe set out above her. This was what really mattered - and this – a panoramic sunset unimpeded by tower blocks.

She turned towards Raff who was taking in all the stunning colours of the sky and realised that there was no one else she would rather share a sunset with. She was pleased that he must have felt the same way to bring her here.

He started forward and led her to a fallen tree, which they sat on while he eased the cork out of the champagne. The cork flew up into the trees with a loud report then there was a fluttering of wings and an angry hoot.

'I think you just shot an owl' she grinned, holding up the glasses.

'It sounds distinctly ruffled but definitely not dead.' he laughed, pouring out the champagne. He held his glass up in the air.

'To you, Sadie.' he whispered.

'Thank you' she blushed, hoping it was too dark for him to notice. She didn't know what to say, there was just something in the way he said her name. She continued quickly 'For showing me the sunset too.'

'To many more sunsets' he said and then they both drank from the glasses. They sat in silence, watching the sky turn to a deep carmine red, the whirling of the disappearing sun making a last magnificent display from just above the horizon. Raff suddenly said 'Ah.', got up and then sat down again, refilling the glasses. He left them both in Sadie's hands.

'Wait there.' he ordered, mysteriously.

She watched as he disappeared towards the caravan. It was dark now the sun had gone down but she felt at ease in this garden. She had come home. A few moments later she saw his dark figure coming back towards her carrying a storm lantern, which he held aloft as he reached her.

'I keep one on either side of the Vardo for when I feel like spending the night in the old homestead' he laughed, setting the lantern at her feet. She knew he occasionally slept there to feel close to his family and to nature. 'I just wanted to give you this.'

He brought a small envelope from his pocket and handed it to her. Sadie opened it in the light of the lantern and gasped.

'My amulet! It looks so clean.' she laughed.

'My jeweller friend cleaned it all up professionally and, like Ned thought, it is gold. I got him to replace the link and put a matching gold chain on for you. Now you can keep her with you. I hope that's alright?' he said, an endearingly worried look on his face.

'Alright?' she whispered, 'It's more than alright, it's perfect. It's just finished a perfect day off...perfectly.' Her English teacher wouldn't have been impressed but Raff looked thrilled.

She tried it up against her, the chain was just the right length, and as she tried to undo the catch, Raff took it from her.

'Here.' he said and did a little circling movement with his hand so she obediently turned around. 'Can you hold your hair up off your neck?'

Sadie obeyed again, feeling very exposed as Raff came close behind her. She could feel his breath against her ear and then the light touch of his hands on her neck. This felt so intimate; she could feel her breath quickening. He fastened it then gently stroked her neck. She moaned softly and with that, he turned her roughly round to face him, his lips pressing against hers urgently. His mouth parted, saying her name and then he held his lips against hers once more as they grasped each other tightly.

Ali's raucous laugh, joined by James' hearty one jolted them both out of their embrace and reminded them that Sadie still had guests. They both reluctantly turned back towards the cottage, reaching it just as most of the remaining guests were filing into the kitchen.

Chapter 33

Most of the guests had drifted off gradually during the evening and Dilly, Ian and Drew now shouted their thanks to Sadie as they set off down the driveway. As soon as Sadie and Raff walked through the French doors, a ruddy-faced Meg ran up to her and enveloped her in a python-like squeeze.

'You'll never guess!' she squawked, tottering unsteadily, 'Em has let me rent Church View Cottage from her for a silly rent, which I'm putting up when I start earning more, which I'm sure will be soon because of your wonderful ideas Sadie, don't you think Em?'

Sadie took a breath and focussed after a few seconds on Em's face, Em raised a bemused eyebrow.

'That's brilliant news Meg' smiled Sadie, giving her another hug, 'and I expect this means that you're moving in with James, Em?'

'No, I thought seeing as you spent all that money doing my new dovecote workshop up, I'd move in there, if that's alright?'

Sadie looked nonplussed for a moment, her mind not having recovered from the evening's most recent events, until Em and James burst out laughing.

'It's not such a bad idea' said Ali 'I'd stay the night there, laying on a chaise longue and looking at the sky through the glass roof.'

'That's an idea' grinned Sadie 'I could rent it out as a holiday cottage and advertise it with the proviso 'with stubborn and cynical aunt included in the rent''

'Don't you dare take away my new workshop' protested Em. 'Anyway, I'm in negotiations to sell my old workshop to the museum to show what Victorian working conditions were like.'

James shook his head fondly and took charge.

'Drink, anyone? Or is it coffee-time yet?'

There was a chorus of 'Drink!' apart from Joanna, who put the kettle on. Raff and Sadie for some reason didn't feel the need for any more alcohol.

Sadie looked around at her friends and gave a satisfied sigh. This is just what she imagined her new house to be. A hub that everyone used as their own and a community, that they felt relaxed in these lovely old surroundings. She hoped that Acorn Cottage became as familiar to them as it felt to her as she watched James opening the fridge to get the chilled sparkling wine out and Joanna reaching in the cupboard for coffee mugs. She saw Em throwing her head back with laughter while bagging one of the comfy chairs near the Aga. It all just felt so homely and Sadie realised that apart from her stays at Em's, she had never felt this before in her life.

Meg was cutting up pieces of the 'Cottage cake' she had made and was busy trying to wrap them in serviettes. George wandered down from checking the kids before squeezing Ali's shoulder and plonking a kiss on her head. Raff, when she first met him had appeared surly and anti-social but it couldn't have been further from the truth. He wasn't as loud and outgoing as some but he was friendly and sociable now, laughing at something Thomas was saying. She felt there was a little shyness there, which he camouflaged well.

Sadie took a closer look at Thomas. His cheeks matched Meg's for ruddiness and he looked more animated than she had ever seen him. He also seemed to be having trouble with his words – did he just say 'constipated' instead of 'consecrated'? One look at Raff, trying hard not to laugh while nodding seriously, told her she had heard right.

Joanna caught her eye and Sadie went over to join her and collect her coffee.

'He's bad enough getting words mixed up when he's sober...' she smiled. Nothing ever seemed to fluster Joanna.

'Hasn't he got a church service in the morning?' Sadie asked her.

'Yes he has. He's just said it's okay because he's written his 'sherman' already and all he has to do is 'read there and stand it'.

'Seriously?' said Sadie, a delighted grin appearing on her face. Joanna nodded wisely

'That's why he doesn't usually drink much – he has alcohol-induced Spoonerisms' Then her serious face changed and they both doubled up with laughter.

There came a crash from the far side of the kitchen and Meg was trying to pick up a broken plate while George rushed over to stop her cutting herself.

'S'okay' came a very loud voice from a usually quiet Meg. 'Ish mine, the plate, acshelly. Brought bread up 'n it. Ish mine, not Sadie's. S'okay.'

Sadie looked across at Em and pulled a 'Is she alright?' face. Em leaned closer to Sadie.

'Ish mine acshelly, the plate' she whispered to Sadie, 'but it's an old one and I don't care. In case you were wondering, James and I are on standby to look after the bakery and café tomorrow with Will. Meg will have all on looking after herself. She's so happy about renting my cottage that I'm not going to curb her enthusiasm, especially as I think it may be the last time she'll drink for a good while after she wakes up in the morning.'

'That's good of you both and I'm sure she'll thank you for it when her head is playing drum solos tomorrow.'

'Well, we all have to learn that there is a price to pay for drinking heavily. Most people do it as teenagers, Meg is a late starter.' Em grinned.

'And by the way Em – 'James and I', it's lovely to hear those words.

'It's lovely to say them too, believe it or not.' said Em, contentedly.

Joanna had put the kettle on again, rightly guessing that more coffees would be needed and Sadie took a seat at the table next to Raff. Funny, raucous and possibly very untrue stories were being bandied about. Everyone was holding forth on every subject under the sun and laughter radiated around the kitchen, bouncing off the walls of the old cottage. Raff grabbed her hand underneath the table and smiled into her eyes. I want it always to be like this, thought Sadie and began to envisage Christmas here with all these wonderful people. It didn't seem too much of a stretch at this moment.

A while later, after more stories and more coffees, someone remarked that it couldn't possibly be nearly two in the morning and people started to leave, albeit reluctantly. They all hugged Sadie and said they hadn't enjoyed themselves this much in ages.

'I can see she'll be a bad influence on this village with her drunken parties.' smiled Em fondly.

'She's an asset to the village' announced Thomas, thankfully managing to say the words correctly. 'New blood.'

He stopped with a hand on the door frame and turned 'No- Ancient blood.' he nodded sagely and wobbled through the door.

Meg had just woken up after falling to sleep on James' shoulder. She was now being propped up, with a silly grin on her face, between him and Em.

'We're staying with her tonight at my - her- cottage. Mainly because I want to see her face when she remembers tonight – if she ever does.' smirked Em.

'You're evil.' laughed Sadie and because she couldn't give her and James a hug because of their propping up duties, she blew them both a kiss and thanked them profusely for everything. George waved as he went upstairs and Thomas managed to make it to Joanna's car of his own volition, although he wavered a bit when he took in a lungful of fresh air. Ali came up and flung her arms round Sadie's neck.

'So glad you came here Sade – and so glad we moved up here too. We're all going to be happy. Happy, happy, happy. Happy ever after. Because you're my best friend.'

'Ali, you're not going to do the 'I really love you' drunken ramble are you?'

'Sade, I really, really love you because you're my besht friend ever.' laughed Ali 'See you in the morning, me old mate.'

She turned round in the hallway and looked seriously at Sadie.

'Bacon sandwiches for breakfast?'

'Of course!' replied Sadie and Ali put her thumbs up in salute.

Sadie turned back to the kitchen with a daft grin on her face which faded when she realised the kitchen was empty. Raff wasn't there. Whisky and Bran were curled up together in a basket in the corner, exhausted after playing games all evening outside. He obviously hadn't wanted to disturb Bran and had left quietly. She sat down on a chair and felt stupidly miserable. Of course he'd gone home, why wouldn't he? Everyone else had and it *was* the early hours of the morning. She knew though, that she was making excuses to herself because she thought at least he would have said goodbye – or even stayed a little longer.

Stop being selfish, she thought to herself. You've had such a brilliant night and you're feeling miserable? Ridiculous. She walked slowly over to the French doors to make sure they were locked. As she reached out, the door was pushed open and she and Raff stared at each other in surprise.

'Were you locking me out?' he said in mock disapproval.

'I thought you'd gone home.' she said, trying not to sound like it mattered.

'Just checking nothing was left outside that shouldn't be. I'll sort the trestle tables out tomorrow.' he explained, his eyes not leaving hers. Then he took her hand and led her out of the door.

'Come on.'

'Where are we going? She didn't really care as long as she was with him.

'To see the stars.' he whispered.

Chapter 34

It really was fairyland, though Sadie, her own private fairyland. There was a clear night sky full of stars and lower down, nearer to the earth, it looked like she had her own stars lining the edges of the garden and hanging in the trees. The moon was bright, adding its own light and enchantment to everything.

The water in the fountain was lit up by a blue solar light, which glowed ethereally as they both passed by. It showed a glow around Brighid's benevolent smile as she held the flame, which now seemed to be beating in Sadie's heart. She couldn't remember ever feeling like this before in her life.

She glanced sideways at Raff as he walked slightly in front of her, pulling her along. She watched his lithe body stride on, his white shirt showing up in the half dark, his black hair moving in the gentle breeze. If she reached out, she could just...

He turned and smiled. 'Should I have brought more champagne?' he asked teasingly.

'I don't think we need it, do you?' she felt brave enough to say. 'I think the next time will be Em's wedding.'

She giggled, mostly because she didn't think she would ever say 'Em's wedding.'

'I'm really pleased for them; it's been a long time coming.' Raff said.

'I didn't even realise at first' admitted Sadie 'I can't believe I missed the signs – but once I did know, you couldn't miss them.'

They were coming up to the caravan. Em studied it.

'It's a shame you can't see the sunset from your caravan.' she mused.

'But you can. From the bed at the back, you can just look out of the window and see the sunset – and then in the morning, I lay there and turn my head, and I can see the sunrise through that window.' and he pointed to the window of the door at the top of the steps.

'Now,' he said thoughtfully, continuing the earlier conversation 'if you don't want alcohol, I can make you a cup of tea?' He nodded towards the caravan.

'In there? Can you make tea in there?' she asked.

He sighed theatrically.

'Sadie, a whole family lived in there at one time and made family meals on the one-pot stove. Your ancestors too, no doubt, when they joined them. Especially your wicked great great-grandmother. They used a campfire as well of course.'

'Can you make campfires too?' she asked, fascinated.

'Yes, have you seen the charred earth in front of the Vardo? Although I have to be honest, this kettle will be boiled on a campus stove.'

She laughed and tutted in mock seriousness.

'But' he added 'the tea will be made in my great-grandmother's best china cups.'

'Will everything…taste okay?' she ventured.

'How dare you?' he laughed and pretended to look offended. 'I told you, I use this place a lot. I filled the kettle up and had a cup of tea on the steps first thing this morning. It helps me think sometimes. It helps me get my life in perspective and when I'm in danger of forgetting who I am, I spend the night here to get back to my roots – to

292

feel at one with my ancestors. Does that sound far-fetched and incredibly new-age?' He gave an embarrassed laugh.

'No it doesn't' she replied. She watched him happily from the steps as he lit a lantern and then disappeared inside the caravan. After a couple of minutes, he poured the tea into two intricately patterned teacups, placed in saucers. She wasn't so happy when he held up sachets of long-life milk but nodded all the same. The interior was lit up with another lantern and revealed the rich materials and furnishings she had seen before, made more exotic by the half-light, which picked out the gold threads.

He carefully passed her on the steps and handed her the tea, sitting down next to her. She could feel his leg pressing against hers.

'As I was saying' continued Sadie 'How can I think it's silly, communing with your ancestors when that's exactly what I feel I'm doing here? This...' and although she meant the Cottage, when she looked into his eyes, it meant much more 'has all seemed like fate. The house and how I managed to buy it at a bargain price so easily – even managing to buy it at all, considering the circumstances. I was lucky the owner had forgotten about it. He didn't say he had, I just knew.'

'Do you think that's because of your ancestors' witch-like all-seeing powers?' he teased, his lips twitching.

'You know it's not. We all have the power of intuition in us and this is what it was. And my family were healers – not witches.' Sadie suddenly thought of the figure she had seen in front of her in the garden, the one she was convinced was Agnes Norwood.

'Although' she said reflectively 'there are more things on this earth that we don't know about than those we do.' She felt for the amulet around her neck and stroked it, sending silent thanks, just in case.

'That was deep, Sadie Norwood.' he laughed and took the empty cup out of her hand, putting it on the ground next to his.

'And you should know me and my family history more than most people, Raff Maguire. They have lived alongside each other for many years.'

Raff pulled her close. Sadie tried to concentrate on what she had just said but it was fading. All she could think about was how good this felt, her face being next to his, breathing the same air.

'Our families have a past together Sadie but I think we have a future.' whispered Raff.

She didn't remember any more except the soft feel of his lips, turning urgent as their bodies melded together and he ran his fingers through her hair. She closed her eyes and held him like she'd never let him go. This is what it feels like then, she was vaguely aware of thinking. After all these years, this is what love feels like.

Raff pulled away and stood up slowly, holding his hand out to her, pulling her gently up.

'Come and see the sunrise with me, Sadie Norwood.' and she followed him inside the caravan, into their past - and their future.